CITY OF SHADOWS

SAINT TOMMY, NYPD - BOOK 4

DECLAN FINN

City of Shadows

Dedicated to Father Brendon Laroche of Allentown PA, and all the other Kickstarter backers who made this one possible.

ACKNOWLEDGMENTS

As always, I would like to thank the Newquists, L Jagi Lamplighter, and Margaret and Gail Konecsni of Just Write Ink for all of the editing. I'd like to thank Jason Garrick for all of the advice about London.

I'd also like to thank all of my Kickstarter backers, and most of all you, the reader, for investing so much into Saint Tommy in the first place. I would especially like to thank you for all of the reviews... you have remembered to leave yours, I hope. Heh.

And, as always, Vanessa. For everything.

1

MISSIONARY POSITION

The one nice thing about temporarily moving to the Vatican was that everyone had finally stopped calling me a saint.

Instead, they called me a wonder-worker. Which I suppose is an improvement.

It had only been two months since I had been brutally beaten and broken at the hands of a warlock. I was up and walking faster than anyone had expected, including myself and my doctors. Some people thought this was great since that meant I would be away and out of the line of fire until I was no longer politically inconvenient. My wife, six months pregnant, was less than thrilled.

My miraculously fast healing concerned me for different reasons. I hadn't spent months praying for God to heal me. I prayed that I may be of most and best use to him. This resulted in my rapid healing and being shipped off to Rome.

This is why, as I sat and waited in a Bishop's office, I was quite concerned about what might be in store for me.

Across from the desk sat Auxiliary Bishop Xavier O'Brien. He was a tall man with graying black hair, slightly ashen complexion, and a cigarette dangling from his mouth. His solid black cassock looked immaculate, despite the ashes all over the desk. His dark brown eyes studied me for a long moment.

"You're the wonder-worker, huh?"

I shrugged. "Apparently, your eminence."

O'Brien waved it away. "Call me XO. Everyone else does. Tell me, what have you done?"

"So far, only the historically verifiable abilities."

XO arched a brow and just gave me a cynical glance over his cigarette. "God-given abilities have been credited for everything from miracles to the ability to litigate a successful tort. You'll have to be more specific."

I sighed. He was being pedantic and picky, but he was right. There were too many people using the words "God-given gifts" a little too casually.

"Thus far, I have been able to manifest several duplicates at once. I have levitated a little. Once, I prayed hard enough that my wife recovered from a slit throat. I have drunk poison without ill effects, aside from a trip to the bathroom. Largely, I can smell evil. And once..." I hesitated at the last one.

XO prompted me with a "come here" gesture.

I sighed. "I once woke up with an angel telling me to smite agents of Satan, right before a SWAT team broke into my house to kill my family and me."

XO nodded slowly. "For the record, those are referred to as charisms or spiritual gifts. I know it's not exactly easy to look up 'what to do if you're a saint' on Wikipedia, but you should get the terminology down if you're going to work here. There's words of wisdom, knowledge, increased faith, healing, miracles, prophecy, etc. In your case, you have the ability to tell the difference between a demon and an angel. You understand any languages you never took classes for?"

I held back my laugh. "I took Latin in high school. I know most romance languages without a problem."

XO rolled his eyes. "You're from New York, all right. Okay, smart ass, do you speak in tongues?"

"Not that I've noticed."

XO nodded, as though he dealt with people like me all the time. "Now, just to be clear, you're part of the NYPD foreign intelligence division, loaned out to us."

I nodded. He apparently didn't want to discuss my abilities in depth. I didn't blame him. I didn't want to talk about it all that often, anyway. "I don't know if it's officially or unofficially, but yes. That would be the case as I understand it. It was one way to get me out of town."

XO nodded. "Good. I'm an old-school Jesuit. Back when being a Jesuit meant that we were loyal directly to the Pope, not whatever crackpot liberation theology guru was hot at the time. That not only means that I have two Doctorates, one in the Philosophy of Science and one in canon law. They mean that details are important to me." XO tapped out the cigarette in an ashtray, reached for another, and continued. "At the end of each mission, we want to send you back home to New York. Whether you go or not is up to you. But I understand you have a daughter on the way."

I nodded, letting him continue.

"It'll do good for you to recharge. We'd fly the family out to you, but as I recall, flying pregnant women is a risky proposition."

I nodded. I wasn't happy being separated from Mariel and Jeremy, but my wife and son understood. Between scrubbing the internet of the million-dollar bounty on my head, and the people who were miffed that their mayoral candidate had been dragged into Hell, I was not the most popular cop in all of New York. And that was with me being a ... well, saint. Metaphorically.

"What's the first step?" I asked. "Are there protocols for me to learn? Is there an immediate threat to look into?"

XO smiled slyly as he lit up. "We'll need you to leave for London tomorrow morning."

I arched my brows, only slightly surprised. I knew I would be sent out soon, the moment I healed up. I hadn't quite thought that it would mean immediately after I had healed.

"What are the particulars?" I asked. "What's there?"

"For your first mission, we thought we'd keep it simple. Armed robbery." XO said, his smile mischievous.

I cocked my head, confused. "Really? From where? A church?" I tried to think of any major *Catholic* churches in London, but I could only think of places that were stolen by King Henry VIII and his contemporaries.

"There's been a break-in at the British Museum."

I nodded calmly, but my mind tried to figure out what it might have been. "And?"

"The stolen object has writing older than anything that anyone has ever seen before. People on the ground are worried. For all they know, it could be something for summoning Cthulhu."

I frowned. Now I was deeply confused. "I thought Cthulhu was supposed to be an Elder god made up by HP Lovecraft."

XO scoffed. "Please. It's a demon without the human meat shield that protects *us* from seeing their horrible visage. Trust me, if you thought an angel of the Lord was terrifying, you should see an angel from Hell. Those who gaze upon them often go mad."

I nodded slowly. There was a moment of silence between the two of us. I waited for him to say something, but he didn't. "Anything else?"

"You'll end up with more data from our people on the ground."

I cocked my head at him. "You have an advance team there already?"

XO smiled. He left his cigarette in his mouth as he spread his arms wide. "We're the Catholic church. We're everywhere you don't want us to be."

I laughed. "I've made that joke myself. So at the end of the day, I'm being sent over there to be a Vatican Ninja?"

XO's gleeful expression faded and his hands lowered. His eyes narrowed and wouldn't meet my gaze. They went ... *shifty* is the only way I could describe it. "Why no .... of course not... we don't have ninjas here. Who do you think we are, anyway?"

I rolled my eyes. "Let's not even have that conversation. I read that book."

XO sighed. "I know. So did a lot of other people. With a book called *A Pius Man*, you'd think it would have been more about our *current* Pope Pius than everything else."

I couldn't disagree with him. But I was perturbed by going into a situation where I would be acting as a spy in a foreign country ... with so little information to start with. I technically didn't care that I was going there as a spy, since the NYPD is the only police department I knew of who had their own foreign intelligence. Though "Vatican Spy" had a nice ring to him.

"That's it?" I asked. "Is that all I need to know?"

XO paused a moment. He took the cigarette out of his mouth, lowered it, and leaned forward. "Let me be clear. You're going to go into a situation where we don't know what the problem is, or why it concerns us. I'm not sure if it's going to tell you anything for your own good to learn that sensitives on the ground are having nightmares so terrifying, they're reporting them to the *Bishops*."

I latched onto one word from all that. "Sensitives? You mean psychics?"

XO shrugged. "After a fashion. Mysticism is a thing, and it's coming back into fashion, Detective Nolan. You're not the only one who's been gifted with charisms. But so far, you're one of the few who can double as an operative."

I scratched the back of my head. I was getting used to the stranger stuff, honestly, but this was a little much. "So I'm going to investigate the theft of a rock because people are having bad dreams?"

XO jabbed the cigarette at me. "Listen, buddy. These are people who have healed many with good intentions and predicted the end of the Soviet Union, and, after that, predicted the oncoming Jihadi threat. They are trying to have a good night's sleep, only to wake up screaming about how the shadows are coming alive to drag the entire city into Hell. There are little old ladies who practically eat, drink, and sleep adoration who are afraid to go to sleep unless they're inside a church, because of the Incubi in their dreams and the scent of brimstone upon waking. There are exorcists who have dispelled demons terrified about towering beasts of black flame that try to devour their souls—*while they're still awake.* So don't even think we're sending you there because you're a simple morale boost. Something. Is. Wrong."

I held my hands up in surrender. "Okay. Thanks. I usually prefer a little bit more to go on. I'll make do."

XO nodded. "Yes. You will. Your contact on the ground will fill you in on everything we have. Besides, you're not going to want nightmares before you get there. Anything else?"

I stood, figuring that this was the end of the discussion. "Yes, I need to know when the next mass is."

XO scoffed. "This is the Vatican. We have hot and cold running masses. You want this evening or tomorrow morning?"

"Both would be preferred."

XO blinked, taken aback. "Really?"

I refrained from rolling my eyes. "I attend daily mass now. I have since my last battle." I shrugged. It was no big deal. "It's an hour a day I don't spend on paperwork."

2

LONDON CALLING

My major problem with my intelligence division assignment was that I wasn't allowed to carry a gun. The only place in Europe I was even allowed to carry a handgun would be Switzerland. In London, it would be worse—no one was even allowed to carry a pocket knife. In fact, I heard people were being encouraged to turn in their kitchen knives.

I spent the plane ride in a state of prayer. I thought about my family. I thought about my partner, Alex, who had bid me a fond farewell barely 72 hours ago. I prayed for everything and everyone I had left behind since I had no idea when I would see them again. I wasn't particularly worried about not surviving. Death happened. If it happened to me, I didn't have anything left to worry about except where I was going. But this was going to be the longest I had been away from my family in years. Since I had been married, I hadn't been away from Mariel for longer than the length of a law enforcement conference. To my surprise, even masses at the Vatican did only so much to mitigate the anxiety I felt about being away from home.

The moment I was in UK airspace, I was jerked out of my state of prayerful meditation. The plane was still at 20,000 feet (and descending), but I was hit with the awful smell that was worse than a field of rotting corpses. I had scented it around MS-13 gangbangers, who had made evil their motto (I submit that "Rape, control, kill" is not something *good*). I had smelled it off of a warlock and in an abortion clinic run by a death cult. The worst had come off a demon.

It was the smell of evil.

It took me by surprise. I felt fortunate I didn't vomit right there. I gagged but fought it down with a combination of willpower and a collection of fast Hail Marys. I didn't mind the discomfort, but I did mind puking on my fellow passengers.

Once my reaction was under control, I did some quick calculations. The most important question was if the source of the stench was on the plane with me. It couldn't have been. I was in the rear of the plane. I would have caught it as I walked the entire length of the cabin. While I wasn't certain of my range, I knew the evil had to be in the general vicinity.

But that means that if it's not on the plane, it's in the city. The entire city.

I shook that thought off. *It can't be the entire city. If something were that evil, it would have probably collapsed under its own weight by now...*

Dear God, this is going to fall under the heading of cheating, but I'm going to have to ask that, if this smell is permeating the entire city, smelling evil is one gift I'm going to have to put aside. I could barely stand a half-hour in the Women's Health Corps main building. If I'm to be any use at all to You in London for any length of time, this smell will either have to turn down or turn off completely. If it is truly as bad as I suspect, then I humbly request—

On my next breath, all I could smell was the stale, recycled air of the plane's cabin.

Thank You, God. Thank You, thank You, thank You.

It didn't occur to me until after a minute of thanking God that it confirmed that evil had soaked into London, perhaps the fabric of the city itself.

The plane rattled and shook as we came in for a landing. We touched down without incident. It took the usual length of two and a half decades of a rosary for us to start to disembark the plane, and it took another decade for me to actually get off the plane. Welcome to the unfriendly skies.

I followed the herd of my fellow passengers to the luggage carousel. It may be considered hubris, but I counted it as a miracle that my bag was the first one off.

There was only one priest at Arrivals. He was of medium height, with a sturdy build. He wore typical black on black on black for his pants, shirt, and jacket. He was bald, mid-forties, with a closely-cropped brown beard. His eyes were brown and warm and friendly, hidden behind glasses with black frames so thick they looked like they had been borrowed from Clark Kent.

He held up a sign that read "Nolan."

I strode up to him and nodded. "Pearson?"

He grinned. "Detective Nolan!" he said cheerfully. "Yes. I am Father Michael Pearson. I am so pleased to meet you. I'm sorry about the mix-up. I thought you were in first class," Pearson told me.

I smiled at him calmly. He was at least friendly. "I was. There was a woman with back problems they were threatening to jam into the rear of the plane. We swapped seats so she could have the bigger chair."

Pearson arched a brow and looked me up and down. I wasn't small. "That was very generous of you."

I shrugged. "Not at all. Once I settle deep enough into prayers, you can cram me into an overhead compartment, and I won't notice. How are we getting around?"

Pearson waved me towards an exit. The sun was up, but I wouldn't call it shining. Even though the sky was clear and blue, it was almost muted, as though someone had put a dimmer on the sun to make it feel overcast.

We headed out to a big black London cab, packed my bag in the back, and slid in. It was dark inside, but roomy. Pearson sat across from me. "The museum or your hotel?" he asked brightly.

"Museum," I said. "Might as well get a start on this."

On the other side of the clear partition, the cabbie nodded and pulled away from the curb as though I had instructed him directly.

Pearson reached behind him and slid the partition closed. "Wouldn't want too much eavesdropping, now would we?"

I nodded. Given what I had dealt with to audition for this job, I couldn't imagine any conversation we'd have that *wouldn't* have us reported to the nearest insane asylum. "No one told me what was happening here. You don't even want to know what I noticed coming in."

Pearson's smile grew, knowing. "You mean the scent of evil so bad you want to cut your nose off? We know. Some of our people here have noticed the same thing. It's so bad for some of them that they've taken to visiting friends in the country just to get away from the stench. Funny enough, once they cross the line for Greater London, the smell goes away." He snapped his fingers. "Instantly."

I frowned. It wasn't unusual for the smell to be bound by a threshold. I always knew it had some limits. "In my experience, it's usually dispelled in the open air. I can't imagine how bad it is that it's reaching me at twenty thousand feet. What's going on here?"

Pearson shook his head. "More than you can imagine. How much do you know about our situation in London?"

I shrugged. "I hear things."

"Knife attacks are up. Violent crime is up. The mayor wants to ban any and all knives in the city, but carry acid? That's a-okay!" His bright, cheery tone faded and grew cynical. "But carrying around containers of acid? That's just ducky. Nearly five hundred acid attacks a year, but why not?"

I cringed. New York City, the most anti-gun city in the United States outside of California, wasn't that idiotic. Single-edged knives were perfectly legal. "What the Hell is wrong with your mayor? Worse, what's wrong with your cops that they're putting up with his crap?"

Pearson sighed, obviously wearied by even thinking about it. "The nanny state, or what we call our government, long ago decided that if national service can't give it to you, you don't require it. This is why there's gun confiscation. Violent crimes are *up*, mind you, but why let reason enter into it. It doesn't help that our mayor is a Muslim communist and most of the rising crime rates are attributed to our 'refugees.' We're told that they 'just can't understand our culture,' given a smack on the bum, and sent on their merry way. Sadly, you can't talk to him as part of this investigation. Maybe you'd be able to talk sense into him."

The laugh came unbidden from my throat. "The last two times I had direct contact with public officials, I sent them straight to Hell. Literally."

Pearson's grin flickered on and off. He knew he shouldn't smile at the thought, but it was obviously coming through. "I had heard something about that."

I looked out the window and watched the city go by. Much of it still looked like it could have easily featured in a Sherlock Holmes movie. Despite the amount of damage during two World Wars, late Victorian buildings were still *de rigeur*. There were the occasional LED or neon lights added, but it was like trying to dress up a concrete bunker with Christmas lights—they were colorful, but it didn't change the nature of the structure. As we went deeper and deeper into the city, certain blocks had statues every twelve feet. There was the stupid giant Ferris wheel, tall spires of London Bridge and Big Ben, giant black taxis, huge, double-decker red buses. Also, I had no idea why they decide to drive in the wrong lane.

"A thousand monuments to past glories," Pearson stated casually. "Most of whom the average man on the street couldn't identify if you gave them a history book, in places they couldn't find on a map if you stuck a pin in it."

I restrained myself from rolling my eyes. New York had its skyline radically altered in 2001, and it felt like half the population had forgotten about it within five years. Almost everyone else had forgotten within ten. Being disappointed that the populace couldn't remember things that happened two centuries ago was laughable.

"I'm almost surprised that there's been little backlash against the stupid policies," I said, getting back on track.

Pearson rolled his eyes. "Our esteemed mayor seems to think that there's a racist backlash coming against the poor innocent refugees ... the ones who are doing it. We won't even discuss Rotherham."

I winced. I knew about Rotherham. It had nothing to do with the recent wave of Middle Eastern refugees. It was far, far worse than that. Rotherham was a place in Northern England that had an entire sex trafficking ring operating there for nearly thirty years without anyone stopping it, despite plenty of evidence. Girls would be kidnapped, disappear into the headquarters, and turned into sex slaves. Fathers of kidnapped children who protested had been arrested. Complaints were dismissed as racist. Cops either ignored reports because they were too lazy to care or on the take from the rapists. I couldn't tell if it was political correctness gone amuck or organized crime to make Al Capone jealous.

The city continued to rush by. The streets seemed darker and shadier. The monuments seemed disapproving of the conversation, scandalized that it would be allowed to happen ... or that people would talk about it.

"Do you think that the smell of evil has to do with the crime rate spiking?" I asked.

Pearson hesitated before speaking. "Only partially. We think it's more the museum than anything else."

"What makes you think that there's a connection between the museum heist and the smell?"

"Because no one really complained about it until the heist two weeks ago. And since the heist, crime has gone up." Pearson frowned. "We are a city of converts, Detective Nolan." He spread his hands in admission. "In fact, I'm one of them. I used to be an Anglican priest. I got better. And when half a million of my flock wanted to come home to Rome, I brought my entire parish over. But like many converts, they're more intense than those born into the faith. Therefore, we have a lot of mystics. I won't say that they're on par with you. We don't have many showing your level of ability. But they're sensitive to things shifting below the surface of the world we can see. And ever since the British museum heist, there were a lot of people in London right now who have A Very Bad Feeling About This."

3

THE MUSEUM

"The museum will be on the left," Pearson told me. I looked over and saw only rows upon rows of late forties apartment buildings. "Behind the apartment buildings."

"You mean it's the next block over?"

"No. Same block, just on the other side of the apartments."

I considered asking why the heck it was going to be *behind* a series of apartment buildings. Almost every large museum I'd ever seen was its own block.

Then again, as the cabbie slowly worked his way through traffic in the narrow, one-way lane, I thought, *Maybe they need the room.*

I was about the make the comment. Then, motion in the corner of my eye caught my attention. I rolled down the window and leaned out to get a better look. It was a collection of at least six young men gathered around a couple. Four of the men were shoving the man between them. The remaining two had cornered the girl against a wall of an apartment building.

The car slowed to a stop because of the gridlock. I grabbed the door handle and popped the door open. "I'll walk the rest of the way."

I slipped out onto the sidewalk and strode up to them. "Excuse me!" I barked in my sergeant's voice. "What are you doing?"

The male victim was given a hard shove, into a wall next to the girl. Three of the men peeled off to confront me. Two stayed with the girl, and a third stayed with the male.

I must not have looked like much. I wore a button down shirt, navy blue blazer, and a light overcoat. It was technically summer, but it was still England. They were a half-dozen young, strong ... Middle Eastern men.

When Pearson said that there were a lot of these attacks, he wasn't kidding. "You pricks deaf?" I barked when I was only twenty feet away and closing. "What do you think you're doing?"

The one in the middle said, "Oi. I think you're in the wrong neighborhood, mate. Shouldn't you be somewhere posh?"

Even though the one in the middle spoke, my eyes were on the one on the right, trying to circle out to the curb. He had a white plastic bottle in his hand, held low and almost entirely behind his thigh.

Acid attacks. Nearly five hundred a year.

I didn't even wait for an attack. I took three large, quick strides. The one with the acid had no time to adjust to my new speed as I drew my knee up, then drove the sole of my shoe into the center of his chest. It was the type of kick to knock down a door. I drove a hammer fist forward into his right clavicle, then drove three fingers above and around his collar bone. Once I had hooked it, I dropped my weight, dislocating the collar bone with a *crack*. Acid Boy screamed, and his grip on the bottle slackened. I held him with my right hand and grabbed the bottle with my left. I didn't even think about it and splashed the contents on the shirts of the other two. As tempting as it was to splash them in the face, permanently marking them, it felt too vindictive.

The other two screamed and ripped their shirts off as they ran down the street, against traffic. Their buddies remained, but not for long. The one on the man tossed him to the ground and bolted to join his friends. However, I grabbed Acid boy and threw him in front of his escape route, crashing the two together. They went down in a pile of arms and legs.

The two men on the girl pulled her away from the wall and dragged her along with them, running away from me.

They might have escaped me if it weren't for Father Pearson, who appeared along their escape route. The good father drove his fist into the face of the first escaping thug. His feet flew off the ground as he fell back, landing in a rumpled heap against the wall.

The last one standing was stunned long enough for me to grab him with a flying tackle. The thug, the girl, and I all went down in a tangle. We crashed to the sidewalk together. The girl screamed and yanked her arm away, scrambling to her feet and up against a wall.

The thug wanted to fight back. I straddled his chest, pinning his arms with my knees. I grabbed his face in both hands and positioned my thumbnails just below his eyes. Since he didn't want me to gouge his eyes out, he stayed perfectly still.

"Hi," I said calmly, only a little out of breath. "I'm new here. Let me introduce myself. I'm Tom Nolan. NYPD. That means I have no authority to actually arrest you guys. However, I'm going to be around for the near future. If I *ever*, and *I mean ever*, find or see any of you six, ever again, I will stop you. Since I can't arrest you, I'll have to find some other way to do exactly that. Am I clear?"

He scoffed. "You'd be arrested," he spat. "You would go to jail. Not me."

I didn't think about my next action. For all I know, I wasn't the one who guided my hand when I reached over and broke his index finger. He gasped. I broke his middle finger and he screamed.

I leaned in and smiled, as though I had meant to do that. "Then report me."

I pushed off of his chest and rose to my feet, dragging him up and hurling him away. All of his friends had long since disappeared.

I turned to the two we had saved and smiled as confidently as I could. I didn't know what had come over me. I hoped I was justified. I generally avoided being brutal with criminals, but something here had set me off. I think I would have felt better had I been aware of breaking the fingers as I did them.

"Thank you," the man said. "I'm Robert."

The brunette offered a hand. "I'm Jillian."

I shook hands with both of them. "Tommy."

Robert nodded. "I can't thank you enough. I didn't want an acid bath and Jill..."

It clicked. The back of my brain had put the pieces together faster than I did. The bottle of acid was to scar Robert. Two men were going to drag Jillian away for what was euphemistically referred to as "a fate worse than death"—though in a post-Rotherham UK, that could have meant one night, or a lifetime. That's why ... *something* in me figured I had to break some fingers to get the point across.

"You might want to head on home? Get off the street?"

Robert smiled, amused. "Working on it." He nodded at me. "Take care of yourself, Tommy."

Jillian and Robert drifted away, walking a different direction from the thugs. I blinked, confused. I looked at Pearson. "I missed a reference, didn't I?"

"They're homeless." Pearson shrugged. "The homeless are more common than you'd imagine." He sighed and walked down the street, picking up my suitcase from the curb. "We have a welfare state second to none, and we have more homeless than anywhere else in the country. Don't ask me."

I sighed. I knew the feeling. New York was much the same, only our homeless were more obviously ... homeless. "How did you get the suitcase out?"

"I paid the cabbie and got the luggage while the traffic was stopped."

We turned the corner... and there was *The* Museum.

If you've seen a museum of natural history in New York or Chicago in America, you've seen the front of the British Museum. It has massive columns at the top of stone steps. Makes it look more like a Greek temple of worship, and you have it pegged. The only difference in this case was the patches of grass leading up to the front steps and the fact that this museum was as big as a college campus at 800,000 square feet. It's dedicated to history, art, and culture, with a collection of eight million pieces gathered during the entire span of the British Empire.

I looked up... and up...and up at it.

"Nice place," I said casually.

New Yorkers abroad did not gawk at anything shorter than a skyscraper, and even then, it had to be an awesome skyscraper.

"We like to think so," Pearson said pleasantly. "Come along."

Even though the design and layout of the museum grounds were awesome, there was damage all over the place. Two of the patches of lawn had gaping holes gouged out of them. There was a chunk of rock blown out of a column that looked like an ice cream scoop had dug out part of it. Crime scene tape had been put up around several areas. Some parts had not yet been marked. Bullet casings were still scattered all over the place. Clusters of concrete rubble were swept off to one side. The back of an apartment building had a massive hole in it. There was a hole where the curb used to be, causing damage to both the sidewalk and the street.

And yet, despite all of the damage, it was still open to the public. The hole in the apartment building was tarped over and strung with crime scene tape. In fact, there was liberal use of crime scene tape everywhere.

Hole in the sidewalk? Crime scene tape. Gouged out patch of lawn? Crime scene tape. Dodgy column? More tape.

"And it's open for business?" I asked.

Pearson waved at the damage, then at the cordoned off perimeters. "We still have some measure of 'stiff upper lip' here. Unfortunately, it typically takes the form of bureaucracy, and the tape is usually red."

"Uh huh... Who went in packing the grenade launcher?"

Pearson shrugged. "Don't ask me. We haven't figured that part out yet. Though what I've seen of the SOCO photos, it wasn't a grenade launcher. They haven't found any fragments or traces of any explosive devices whatsoever."

I walked along the path to the main steps, frowning. Whoever had led the heist had no problem throwing around explosions like candy. If the Scene of the Crime Officers hadn't found anything like an explosive, or fragments thereof, who knew what these guys were working with.

Pearson walked me through the long marble hallways of the British Museum. It's quite obvious that they were trying to split the difference between a museum and a palace.

But the museum exhibits weren't what interested me. The bullet casings, the holes in the walls caused by strafed automatic fire, did.

We were in the Egyptian exhibit when the shootout got really interesting. One central case in the middle of the floor was shattered. The surrounding hall was shot to pieces—instead of the occasional lines of bullets, entire areas were machine-gunned, with the occasional artistic spots of blood.

I frowned, looking around. "What the heck? Seriously, Pearson, what was stolen?"

A new, imperious voice from behind me answered the question. "Only the most important pre-historical artifact anywhere."

The newcomer speaker was a late-middle-aged man, with blonde hair that was starting to go gray. His eyes were half-closed as if he were so bored he might well fall asleep in the middle of the marble hallway. He was tall and thin, and his small smile looked mildly amused at ... something.

Next to him was a brunette with dark curly hair. She was shorter and squatter than he, but seemingly more awake. However, I wasn't going to put anything past anyone. Welcome to London.

I offered my hand. "Thomas Nolan. And you are?"

His smiled flickered. "I am Lord Newby Fowler," he said imperiously, as though his name and title were the most precious things he had. He gave a little bow and gestured to the woman. "And this is my wife, Dame Polly Toynbee."

Toynbee nodded at me simply and curtly. Neither one shook my hand, and I merely let it drop.

"So, what makes it so important?"

Fowler's smile lengthened a little, a lazy cat who already had his prey. "Obviously, you didn't read the card."

I glanced at the plaque underneath the shattered case. It had also been strafed. The description was mangled, though the photograph was intact.

Instead of pointing that out, I said, "I just got here."

Toynbee smiled, also tolerant. "Before we answer any of your questions, perhaps you would like to explain how you got in here, what you're doing here, and why a priest is carrying your luggage?"

Since I didn't know how Pearson had gotten us through the crime scene without being stopped once, I decided to answer the questions I knew. I drew out my shield case and flashed both my badge and ID card. "Detective Nolan, NYPD intelligence division. There are concerns about your missing artifact being at the core of an upcoming terrorist attack. Father Pearson here is a specialist in the fields of Egyptology and archaeology and has been volunteered to be my assistant in this case."

Toynbee and Fowler exchanged a look that I couldn't interpret. Toynbee said, "Ah. So you think that this will be used to *finance* an attack? On New York."

Pearson stepped in for me. "Something like that."

Fowler shrugged. "I suppose that makes a certain amount of sense." He looked me up and down. "Just don't get up to any cowboy antics while you're in our fair city. You wouldn't want to upset the bobbies, now would you?"

I nodded. "Of course not."

"Hmmm.... Come along, Polly. Let's leave the detective to his business. Though we expect to be kept apprised of any news of *our* stone. We spent a pretty penny securing it."

"Of course."

The two of them kept an eye on me until they moved into the next room.

Pearson leaned in. "Terrorist attack?" he whispered. "And just how *did* you know my specialty?"

I looked at him and said in a whisper, "I didn't. I don't know anything about a terrorist attack either. And no, I didn't make it up either. My mouth ran away without me. I suspect God slipped me that script."

Pearson cocked his head. "Does that happen often?"

"Usually not."

"This is going to be *so much fun*," he snarked.

4

LEVERAGE

I looked back the way Toynbee and Fowler left. "Though I should ask, *our* stone? You'd think he made it personally. Did they dig it up or something?"

Pearson shook his head. "They spent a *lot* of money to get it out of customs. No one is quite clear on how or why it came about, but they're apparently well connected. They were both called in on examining evidence and artifacts taken from Iraq. They donated it to the museum. Though whether or not it still belongs to them is a question they never answer directly."

I frowned and furrowed my brow, sparing him a glance. I felt this compulsion to keep my head on a swivel. While the great marble hallways were lit with enough track lighting and glass walls and skylights, I had this strange prickling sensation all along my spine and scalp. It was as though I was covered in crawling bugs. If that was what the comic books referred to as a danger sense tingling, I didn't want it. I had to restrain a shiver, despite all the temperature control.

I hadn't felt something quite so dark since a demon infested my house.

"Was it taken from an Iraqi museum?"

"Worse—one of Saddam's palaces. It was kept in a basement torture chamber."

He had my full attention now. "But you called it an artifact. I didn't know he collected any."

"Oh, but this one was special." Pearson paused and frowned. "Technically, they're all special. We never mentioned the various and sundry objects that Saddam pilfered from his own museums, though plenty got lost in the vast collection of actual looters, museum employees who stole their own exhibits to protect them from rioters, and government officials who just wanted a bauble for the mantelpiece. But this one had a special *purpose* to it. When it was found in the palace, it was bagged up with the rest. But there were notes that came along for the ride. You see, Thomas, this is supposedly from the capital of First Dynasty Egypt. The location was never discovered, but the notes, the legend behind it, is that this stone wiped the city from the face of the Earth."

"The capital?" I paused for a moment. "Didn't they dig that up in the first *Indiana Jones* movie?"

Pearson rolled his eyes. "Americans," he sighed.

I ignored him to lean down to look at the image on the pedestal. It was a rock. It was a very pretty rock. In fact ... "Is that a black diamond?"

"Maybe. No one could sample anything off of it, so it could be obsidian. It could be a diamond."

I frowned deeper. It was beautiful, in a goth sort of way. It was like a black, Satanic Faberge egg. "I need a blow-up. I'm not even certain what I'm looking at."

Pearson smirked, crossed his arms, and leaned up against the pedestal. "You're not the only one, mate. Trust me, it gets weirder."

I chewed on the inside of my cheek, analyzing exactly what I saw. It was egg-like but not as smooth as stone. It was multi-faceted, like a modern cut gem. "Nice knife work."

"'Tisn't a knife."

I straightened. "What do you mean?"

"That diamond has never been cut by man or beast. Not even

mother nature did it. There isn't a single sign of a tool mark on the entire stone. I—here, wait a moment."

Pearson pushed off of the case, strode a few paces, and looked off a split in the hallway. He reached over and came back with a pamphlet for tourists, opening the tri-folded paper. It was clearly the draw since it took up an entire page. Large font proclaimed it THE SOUL STONE.

It was brilliant, translucent, and dark. The very sight of it filled me with dread. There were natural, almost fluid striations on either side, within the stone itself. They were clearly below the gleaming, faceted surface. One set of striations were blood red. The other set was a startling silver. If they weren't *embedded* inside of a millennia-old diamond, I would have thought they were runes.

"Soul stone?" I asked. I would have laughed, but nothing about the implications of that name filled me with cheer.

Pearson nodded. He tapped the facets on the soul stone image. "What you saw is what in the diamond industry is called a rose cut. Or it would be if it had a flat bottom. The thing is, the technique is only around for over a century. But we know it's far older than that because of the striations."

"How do you figure?"

"Because it's a language that no one has ever seen before. It predates ... everything. Yet there are no tool marks on the stone. There's no way that this should exist. The soul stone is entirely impossible. If one didn't know any better, it would be as if it were done by aliens."

I scoffed. "Thanks. I watched that History Channel show. Once."

"Can't blame a guy for having a laugh."

I looked around at all of the random gunfire all over the walls. "Did the action *start* here? I would have thought that we'd see more bullet holes on the way out than at the starting point."

"I didn't bring you here the way they left, believe it or not. I'll save that for the walk-through."

"Let's start. I like to get a chain of events on what happened."

During the night of the robbery, Harrods Department Store had been bombed. This wasn't terribly uncommon. Harrods was to department stores as the King David Hotel was to tourist resting places—the most bombed in the world. Harrods was first blown up frequently by the IRA. Now the jihadists had taken over the job. The world of terrorism is not a very subtle place. You may have noticed that from... almost any actual terrorist attack. Subtle terrorists are television villains.

As Harrods burned, fifteen minutes later, the shooting started here. Over two dozen perpetrators opened up around the soul stone. They whipped out AK-47s from underneath raincoats and screamed *Allahu Akbar* before the bullets flew. Half the bullets went into the ceiling and the other half into the surrounding area. The case was blown up with a length of det cord wrapped around a strip of Semtex. It was looped around the case, secured, detonated. The camera around it was shot out, then the stone was taken. It took them over twenty seconds to get to the next nearest camera, only twenty feet away. Why? According to one bystander who was playing dead, the man who grabbed the stone screamed. He dropped to one knee. The bystander couldn't tell the difference between agony or joy in the scream.

Either way, it only lasted a few seconds. They were on the move, with the occasional shots to encourage people along. Security largely didn't get in their way, since they didn't have the manpower or firepower to stop them.

Then there were the scorch marks.

Apparently, two guards had tried to intervene. Charles Woods and Stuart Preston.

The camera didn't quite catch what had happened. Woods and Preston got in the way of the advance. They had jumped to the front of the caravan of thieves, going melee immediately.

On the cameras, the leader pointed the stone at the guards. The cameras suffered from a massive burst of static. When they came back clear, Woods and Preston were gone, as were the thieves they fought.

All that remained were two shadows, burned into the wall.

Pearson and I stopped for a long moment. I didn't have to study the shadows for more than a moment to realize that they were shadows of four men struggling in hand-to-hand combat.

We kept going.

When the thieves got to the front door, that's when the fun started. The police barricade formed outside. Sure, the Harrods bombing had sucked up the majority of the resources, but this was *The* Museum. Even if it wasn't the primary museum in all of the UK, it was still *huge*. It took them more than ten minutes to get through it at a dead run. By then, the police had figured out that Harrods was a distraction, and sent over a dozen police cars to the scene of the action.

Then it got weird.

The thieves had opened fire on the police, but only a short burst before the heavy artillery opened up ... on the police.

No one saw it, but they presumed at the time that it had been a grenade launcher. The first detonation blew off part of a front column of the museum. The second blew up the back wall of an apartment building. The next few blasts created craters in the sidewalk and the lawn.

Then the police got hit.

The first blast to hit the mark punched a hole *through* a police car, igniting the gas tank *after* the men hiding behind the car had been killed. The second blast slammed into the car like a fist. That car skidded sideways, running over the officers hiding behind it. Once the guys on scene realized that their own cars were of no use, the only option was to hold the scene until the AFO showed up

You are probably aware that the police in the UK are unarmed. In case you're wondering, there are few gun deaths ... but far more violent crimes committed with every other weapon under the sun. It's why one had to be 18 years old to buy a steak knife. It's moronic, but no one asked America. What you probably didn't know is that they're not totally brain damaged. They do have "authorized firearms officers (AFO)." However, out of the thirty thousand cops in the Metropolitan police force, only five thousand officers *in the entire country* were allowed to carry guns.

Looking back at it, even without the deployment of the primary explosive weapon, the responding police force didn't stand a chance.

"How did I not hear about this attack?" I asked.

Pearson sighed. "You have freedom of the press in America. Here, we don't have that luxury. Anything not in the public interest could be locked down without any consequences."

I frowned as I inspected the damage against the column. Half the stone was blasted away, as though by the explosion. The part closer to the door—closer to the shooter—seemed ... melted.

"Father, you see this?"

Pearson frowned at it through his beard. "That's odd."

I nodded as I trotted down the stairs. I darted over to the nearest divot in the dirt. It was exploded, yes, but the crater was half glass. Same with the impact points for the sidewalk and the street.

"Did anyone notice that these impact points look like something from ... I don't know? A science fiction plasma gun?"

Pearson frowned. "No. Most everyone else was busy being shot at."

I frowned. "How much progress have the police made into this?"

Pearson hesitated. "Not much..."

I arched a brow. There were moments that I was tempted to see if I could read minds, like wonder workers before me ... except those incidents had been in or around a confessional. While a combination of smelling evil and reading minds would have made my job easier, it would have felt awkward asking God to do everything but make the perpetrator light up like a neon sign.

Instead, I would have to settle for pulling teeth the old fashioned way. "I've come a very long way. I took a nonstop flight, so I was in a chair for nearly five hours. Holding back on me at this point? Not a good idea. Just tell me."

"Two of the thieves were killed during their escape. They've both been identified. They were from the East London Mosque."

I considered everything he said on the way in. "Let me guess, no one has talked to their friends? Their families? Their Imam?"

"Oh, they don't have any family," he said airily. His tone turned darker as he elaborated. "They were refugees from Syria."

I rolled my eyes. I didn't care who the perpetrator was. When cops had a suspect—or better, the dead body of the perp—the investigator should talk to every friend, family member, and coworker of the diseased. If a cohort was at large, the odds were better than even that the accomplice was among that list, somewhere.

I perked up ... for a moment. "Wait. What about MI-5? Aren't they independent of the Met police?"

Pearson smiled. "True. I could put out some feelers."

I nodded. "Indeed. This would be the point where I should ask how exactly you've done all of this and how you gained all of this data."

Pearson merely smiled. "I wasn't always a priest."

"I figured that out when you punched the thug in the street."

Pearson kept smiling. "I'll see what I can find. But first, we should probably get you checked in and settled for the night."

On the one hand, the sun was still up and shining. On the other, it still seemed ... muted. The shadows seemed longer than they had any right to be. I tried to do the math, but I had jumped time zones twice in the last three days. I was on the road to the airport at nine in the morning in Rome. My flight left at 11, took four and a half hours, another half-hour to get off the plane, and another half-hour to drive from the airport to *The* Museum. After examining the crime scene, it should have been 5:30, maybe six.

"You have a deal," I told him.

"Great. On the way, I can tell you all about the legends of the soul stone."

I arched a brow. That was a strange way to put it. "How many are there?"

Pearson shrugged. "Only two. We did just find it after all. Toynbee and Fowler have dismissed the original legend. I think they prefer it as an alien artifact."

"What's the original?"

"Oh, that it was given to the first pharaoh by Anubis, the Egyptian god of the dead himself. And if it were ever misused, it would annihilate any who use it."

I rolled my eyes. *Great. I've entered an Indiana Jones movie. I hope no one tries nuking a refrigerator while I'm here.*

5

ECUMENICAL DISCOURSE

A pparently, during the summer, the sun doesn't really go down until well after ten at night. Closer to eleven, actually.

Despite that, no matter what I did, or where I walked, or what angle I looked at the city, the shadows seemed to be long and dark and deep. It was the sort of day where I would look out the window and conclude that it was overcast, and we were in for nothing but rain. Everything I have seen or heard about London should have prepared me for that. Except, there wasn't a cloud in the sky since I arrived.

The hotel I was in was ... old fashioned. How old fashioned? The keys look like something you'd see in a medieval castle, only three inches long instead of a foot. The room was on the top floor, so the ceiling was slanted, to match the roof.

When I checked in, the room was dark, despite the sun shining directly through the window. There was that one bright spot in the room. The sun only penetrated six feet in and stopped.

Maybe it was the smell of evil that covered the city like a blanket so thick that I had to ask God to turn off my sense of smell. Maybe it was that it felt like they had put a dimmer switch on the sun. Perhaps

I had spent too many weeks jumping at shadows ... perhaps because I'd fought a warlock who had tried to feed me to shadows.

No matter the reason, I turned on all the lights in the hotel room. They were all turned on high. I still felt like I slept in the pitch dark. I prayed myself to sleep.

I usually don't dream. But that night, I did.

And they were nightmares. There were living shadows that tried to eat my soul. To flee them, I ran into a burning building. My coat caught fire without slowing me down. Then my skin burned. I tried to run upstairs, but they gave way. Then so did the floor.

Basically, it felt like I was living in a Lovecraft novel.

At the heart of the dream was the soul stone itself...a black, rose-cut oval obsidian piece with red and silver striations within the surface. The striations formed deliberate glyphs that should be indecipherable, but I was certain I could read it. The rose cut and the glyphs had no tool marks as if it were naturally formed that way...

At that, I shot out of bed. I resisted the urge to clear under the bed and in the closet. It was tempting. But I didn't. Jeremy didn't even do that, and he was 10.

I slowly lowered myself back to the bed, closed my eyes, and prayed for a little more sleep before—

Then my alarm went off.

"Of course," I murmured.

I rolled out of bed and onto one knee, for my daily prayer. It was from another Saint Thomas— Aquinas.

Grant O merciful God, that I may ardently desire, carefully examine, truly know and perfectly fulfill those things that are pleasing to You and to the praise and glory of Your holy name. Direct my life, O my God, and grant that I might know what you would have me to do and for me to fulfill it as is necessary and profitable to my soul. Grant to me, O Lord my God, that I may not be found wanting in prosperity or in adversity and that I may not be lifted up by one nor cast down by the other. May I find joy in nothing but what leads to You and sorrow in nothing but what leads away from You. May I seek to please no one or fear to displease anyone, save only You.

Grant to me, O Lord God,

—a vigilant heart that no subtle speculation may ever lead me from You;

—a noble heart that no unworthy affection may draw me from You;

—an upright heart that no evil purpose may turn me from you.

Give me a steadfast heart that no tribulation may shatter and a free heart that no violent affection may claim as its own.

And finally, grant me O Lord my God, a mind to know you, diligence to seek you, wisdom to find you.

Give me a way of life pleasing to You; perseverance to trust and await You in confidence that I shall embrace You at the last. Amen.

As usual, I felt better after saying it and went about my day.

Once the restaurant fed me, I was out the door and headed for mass at Westminster Cathedral. It was not only Roman, but it was also where Father Pearson worked.

It was located in Central London, a highly modern part of the city. It was near Century House, the new home for MI-6, seen in the later James Bond films, from Brosnan to Craig. The entire area is a mass of silver and glass. And when you walked past some of the glitz, there was Westminster Cathedral. And it is pretty and very neo-Byzantine. While the main building is around five or six stories high, the spire is easily twice that. The floor was around 54,000 square feet, so that gives you an idea of how big it is. There were no flying buttresses on the outside. It was built of brick and concrete. The exterior broke up the red brick with white stone bands. The bricks were even hand-molded. The main entrance facade had a deeply recessed arch over the central entrance, flanked by tribunes and stairway turrets.

Outside was the plaza. The plaza itself was tiled, the gray stones running diagonally to the cathedral. The plaza was hemmed in by steel and glass buildings on either side. It looked like the 21st century had come crashing in on the 1890s and they were trying to live together amicably.

The problem came when you went halfway down the plaza. When I arrived for mass, there was a small gathering of a dozen people in front. They were yelling at parishioners as they tried to pass.

If you are automatically presuming that the gathering all happened to be young men of swarthy complexions, beards and wearing a variety of Middle Eastern headgear, you'd be right.

The ones I was concerned about were holding plastic bottles like the acid container I saw on the way to the museum.

Aw nuts.

I looked around. Two policemen were standing on the corner, doing nothing. I remembered Father Pearson talking about ignoring crimes because of the perpetrator being of X or Y disposition, but it was hard to believe that policemen would just *sit* there as innocent bystanders were assaulted.

Since the acid could have opened up at any minute, I knew I couldn't walk around the buildings and flank them. I walked straight for them, in the center of the line, which was what everyone else was avoiding.

I prayed quickly. I didn't know what to pray for, so I simply asked God to grant me whatever would best suit the situation. I didn't care if He levitated me over and behind the line of thugs, or if He bi-located me several times so I could take them on one-on-one. Or if He gave me nothing at all ... that would be the only thing I wouldn't quite know how to work with.

So, of course, I received ... nothing.

Okay, Lord...let's see how this works.

I walked up to the leader. He had only just started on his beard, and it wasn't quite groomed properly. If he was twenty, I'd be surprised. He wore a white Taqiyah (a Muslim Yarmulke) and a black t-shirt in Arabic script. I wouldn't be surprised if it translated to *Rage Against the Machine.*

How did I know he was the leader? He looked at me, made eye contact, and didn't look away. Everyone else looked forward to attacking several of the parishioners who had hung back. That was good. I didn't want them keeping their eye out for any parishioners who circled around.

I stopped a mere four feet away. The men with the acid bottles were spaced out on either side of the leader. Every other person had a bottle. *Aw nuts.*

I smiled at him calmly and casually. "I'm giving you one chance to leave before this gets messy," I said conversationally.

He sneered. "Really, infidel? You *threaten* me? You *give* me *anything*? The police fear me. The *government* fears me. Touch me, and the city *burns.*"

I rolled my eyes. "You? No. Mass rioting? Yes. Now get going before you have a problem."

The leader laughed. He looked to the men on either side of him. "You think you can defeat all of us?"

I shrugged. "I may not have to. You want to see how many hang around after I beat you and your two closest companions into the dirt?"

"All of us?"

While I kept my eyes firmly locked on the leader, I wasn't actually looking at him, but tracking everyone else with my peripheral vision.

"Listen closely to how I'm speaking. Do I sound like I care?"

The leader's eyes narrowed. He reared back and roared. "You're American!"

"From New York."

The leader gave a slight nod. The acid holder on the left took a step forward, his bottle arm cocked and ready.

I shot forward and grabbed the leader by the shoulders. I yanked him forward and ducked behind him and shoved the leader into the path of the acid. The splash and sizzle of acid on flesh told me that the acid thrower had shot his wad. I took a step back with my right foot and spun the leader around, shoving him into the other acid bearer. They tumbled down to the pavement together. The second acid bottle popped open, splashing the bearer in the side of the face.

I swung back the other way, punching the thug that had stood on the leader's left.

I continued the spin, snapping a kick into the side of the knee of the man who had been on the leader's right. The knee buckled. I spun back with a hammer fist straight to the nose.

I jumped over the fallen fourth thug, my fist cocked by my ear. I hit the next thug with the entire force of my body weight, punching through the target. His head snapped back with a small spray of blood. I grabbed the empty acid bottle out of his hand. I stepped past him with my right leg, hooking behind his, and swept the leg out from under him.

The next thug seemed shocked. I tossed the empty acid to him. He flinched and caught it. I promptly kicked him in the chest, knocking him back into another acid-wielder. That was six down and a seventh inconvenienced.

I shot to one side, closer to the church. I both wanted to show them that I had clearly passed their barricade and give them a moment to consider that I had just dropped half of their number.

The remaining six had three acid bottles between them. That seemed to tip the balance in their thought process. All three of the acid wielders unscrewed the bottle tops.

Okay, Lord, what's the next step?

Out of the side, behind the McDonald's, a black streak shot out, plowing into the nearest acid-wielder, smashing down on the wrist with the acid. The attacking arm came back up in a blade hand that slammed into the thug's throat. It made him gag and fall back, trying not to choke.

The black blur was Father Michael Pearson. He shoved the gagging man aside.

I decided to chance it and charged them, screaming.

The remaining thugs ran away, dropping their acid on the pavement.

After they turned the corner, I doubled over, hands on my knees. My heart rate had spiked. And I hadn't even noticed it during the fight.

Dear God. I'm glad You have as much faith in me as I do in You. Though it would have been nice if You sent Pearson earlier. Just saying...

I took a breath and stood. Pearson had wandered over and waited for me to catch my breath.

"Stressful morning, is it?" he asked.

"Just a little. Who knew it would be this hard to get to mass in the morning."

Pearson rolled his eyes. "Tell me about it. Come on, mass is about to begin."

AFTER MASS WAS a trip to the other side of the River Thames, to Thames House on 12 Millbank. It had a very nice view overlooking the river, a rock's throw from the Double Tree by Hilton.

According to Pearson, the building was constructed in 1930 on riverside land, cleared after a flood in 1928 had damaged multiple run-down residential properties. Thames House was built by the Government's Office of Works, which is why it was a near carbon copy of Imperial Chemical House down the road. It had once housed International Nickel Ltd. and even the Northern Ireland Office. It was owned privately until it was sold to the British Government in 1994.

The design was 'Imperial Neoclassical'—which looked like they just wanted to take Victorian England and smash it up a bit with the Roman Empire.

MI-5 had moved into Thames House in the late 1980s, due to their previous headquarters being 1) all over the place (with headquarters, technical services, and administration being in two different places) and 2) falling apart. In 1989, Thames House had just been vacated by the Department of Energy, so the timing worked out.

Thames House wasn't *that* far from Westminster, so Father Pearson and I legged it. Along the way, he explained to me the history of the location.

To be honest, it was not the most impressive building I've ever seen. It ate up the whole block like it was trying to be the museum, but the shining tower of glass and steel next to it was more impressive, even to a New Yorker like myself (though after 9-11, I honestly prefer steel and concrete, like the Empire State Building).

Though the most distinctive part of Thames House was the archway in front, which felt more like a massive maw, ready to devour all.

"Subtle," I told Pearson.

"Isn't it though? Come along. We have an appointment."

We were met at the front door by someone who was, generously speaking, the epitome of "bureaucrat." He was a little gray man in a little gray suit, vest, and tie. His thinning hair was gray. Even his eyes were gray.

He offered me his hand and said, "Griseo Grayson. My coworkers call me Gris."

I did not laugh at his name. Honest I didn't. Especially when you realized that "griseo" meant "gray" in Latin. I didn't ask him if he came out of the womb with the color palette of a 1940s Cary Grant movie. Though it was close.

Coworkers? Most people call them "friends." I smiled and said, "So, how much do you know about what we're here for?"

Grayson gave a sad little smile. He waved us down the hall and said, "Let's find some more private quarters to have this conversation, hmm?"

We followed him down the marble halls. Much to my surprise, we didn't change floors. We didn't even go far. Instead, we ended up in the men's restroom.

Grayson entered first, then came back to get us. "Come in," he whispered. "You can't trust anyone here. This is a house of spies, after all. And there are more politics in this building than there is spying."

The small bathroom was five stalls wide. Grayson leaned up against one of the sinks. He crossed his arms and frowned. "The official answer of MI-5 is that there is nothing interesting about the dead thieves from the East London Mosque."

I arched a brow. "And unofficially?"

Grayson's frown didn't shift much. He pursed his lips pensively. "We're not allowed to even look at a mosque. Even after the London attacks in 2014, any surveillance on ... any Muslim whatsoever ... results in harassment and racism charges."

I blinked once, hard, then shook my head in confusion. "Wait, what about watch lists? What are those for?"

Grayson rolled his eyes and sighed. He shook his head sadly. "So we can tell the media that we had some idea of what was going on before all Hell broke loose. How many different terrorist attacks have you seen in the news where the statement afterwards claims they were on a watch list? And yet, no one seems to be watching them. Because if we even go *near* a mosque, or a London resident who's Muslim, the mayor of London blows our cover, then feeds the surveillance team to the mob. The Mayor has decided because he's Muslim, it means that self-defense is Islamophobia. He bans ownership of kitchen knives, but not acid. So we have nothing."

I looked at Pearson. He said nothing, just shrugged. He told me so but apparently figured that I wouldn't believe him unless I heard it straight from the source. I frowned, then looked at Grayson. I hoped to get *something* out of this encounter, despite knowing that there were more than enough dead ends in any investigation.

"If MI-5 were allowed to investigate," I said, "how do you think you'd go about it?"

Grayson's eyes finally lit up in amusement. "I don't know if you're aware, but the two men found at the Museum were Syrian refugees. They had no friends. They had no family. The only thing they had? East London Mosque. They lived there. They associated with no one outside of there for months."

I nodded slowly. "Thanks. I guess we should have a talk with the Imam."

Grayson nodded. He pushed off the sink. "I think we understand each other fine." He headed for the door, then stopped. He looked back at us. "Do you know how the CIA spies on Americans who they suspect of international espionage?"

I paused a moment. "I know that they don't call the FBI."

Grayson actually smiled. "They call MI-6, and *they* bug the

Americans for the CIA. Think of it as a similar matter of outsourcing intelligence work." With that, Grayson left.

I looked at Pearson. "Are things really that bad around this city?"

Pearson looked at me over his glasses. "What were you saying about the last time you dealt with *your* city's mayor? You sent him straight to Hell?"

"Point taken."

It was four miles and a half-hour between Thames House and the East London Mosque. Half of that time was a twelve-minute walk to the nearest train station, a fifteen-minute ride on an "underground" so cramped that it made a New York City subway ride feel like a luxury yacht, and walking seven minutes to the Mosque itself.

Also, it took an hour to get there. Had I known that the homeless were so common, I would have converted more money. Since my salary was paid by the NYPD, and my room and board were being paid for by the Vatican (hence the cheap accommodations), I didn't bother to carry a lot of cash on me. Since Pearson was on the same Vatican pay tab, he didn't have loose cash, either. However, he had a lot of business cards for the Cathedral and Catholic services. I handed out one to every homeless person we met. Then I gave out more for their friends. Then I asked Pearson about staying in the Cathedral rectory so they could save money on my room and board at the hotel.

Welcome to the welfare state—it just made more poverty.

As we came up from the subway platform, I was sure that my mind played tricks on me. The area was ... relatively undistinguished. It wasn't as fancy as anything around the center of town, but it didn't look any worse than my hotel. In fact, if it reminded me of anything, it reminded me of Main Street, Flushing, in Queens. The only real difference that stood out was that, instead of the Chinese of Flushing, it was the Bangladeshis of Whitechapel. Yes, Whitechapel, home of Jack the Ripper.

So that's why I was absolutely certain my mind played tricks on me. Once more, the street felt far too dark to be late morning. It was as though the sun were scared to come out and rear its visage upon the world, and endless night seemed only a few days, if not hours, away.

As I said, the very knowledge of it being the area of Jack the Ripper colored my perception.

The mosque itself looked more like a library on Whitechapel Road.

According to Pearson, the three-story mosque was built in 1985, on land *still* left empty from bombing in World War II. The exterior was brick of beige, with light red brick trim. The mosque was capped with a large golden dome, but you couldn't see it from the front of the building. It had three minarets—two small ones were on either side of the main entrance, and the main one seven stories off the ground. It was of a piece with the even larger London Muslim Center on the right, and an even *larger* hall.

It was church, gym, rec center, and school all in one stop.

"Funny," I muttered. "Jam all of that together in New York, and you'll be arrested."

Pearson scoffed. "No comment."

We walked into the mosque.

6

INTERFAITH DISCUSSIONS

We had only walked into the East London Mosque. We hadn't even gone four feet past the door before we ran into the Imam.

Imam Abu Hamza Kozbar was a big man, somewhere around the size of a rugby fullback. His full black beard came down to his diaphragm. His cassock was solid white, complete with matching Taqiyah.

Kozbar had been talking to a small gathering of his followers when we walked in. We caught his eye. Pearson's priest outfit probably gave him a clue that we were not members of the congregation.

"What are you doing here!" he barked.

Kozbar came in and raised his right hand to shove me in the chest. I knocked his hand aside with my left hand, pinned it against his chest with my right, and grabbed his bicep with my left.

"Hi. I'm Tom Nolan. We'd like to ask you about some of your parishioners."

The Imam looked me up and down, sizing me up. The gears behind his eyes ground heavily away as he calculated whether or not he could take me in a fight, followed by contemplating if it was worth the time and trouble to find out.

Kozbar scoffed and pushed me away. "Fah! Under what authority? You're no policemen." He glowered at Pearson. "Not with a priest in tow, and that accent."

"I am an inquiry agent sent in by a private party, concerned about the retrieval of the Soul Stone artifact from the British Museum. Father Pearson is a specialist in archaeology." Which was perfectly true.

The Imam grimaced. "They sent an American?"

I shrugged. "I'm neutral as far as any and all local politics are concerned. The only thing my employer cares about in this instance is the return of the stone. That's it. No one cares about whatever problems you and London have."

Kozbar loomed over me, obviously reconsidering testing my mettle. But he sighed and waved it away. "Bah. All because the two were from my mosque. Would you harass priests if they were Catholic?"

I smiled. "In a heartbeat. But you haven't even begun to see me harass someone yet. The first step in any manhunt is to find people they know. But they knew no one. According to our best sources, they didn't associate with anyone outside the mosque. They had no friends, no family, no other associates. Therefore, we have to start somewhere. Point us somewhere else, we can go there and *harass* someone for real."

Kozbar's eyes narrowed. "I serve seven thousand of my fellow Muslims. I cannot be expected to track all of them, or be invested in their affairs."

I looked to Father Pearson, confused, then back to Kozbar. "How many people are you hosting who live in the complex?"

Kozbar shrugged. "Two hundred? We have a lot of room."

I kept my face placid, but internally, I cringed. In Europe, one of their major concerns with Islam has been their tendency to riot. Whether it be for perfectly sound reasons (where Algerian emigres have been in France for decades, but aren't allowed to assimilate) to rioting at the drop of a hat (political cartoons), as a cop, all I could think was *How many people does it take to start a riot?* Almost any historian worth his salt could answer: *If the conditions are right? One kid with a rock.*

Given the way we were greeted, I decided against asking Kozbar to investigate the refugees he sheltered. If saying hello was cause to nearly get me shoved through the front door, asking this Imam to do ... anything ... would probably end in a full brawl.

"Who would know about the two perps?" I asked.

Kozbar's eyes widened. "Perps? You would call two members of my Mosque as *perps*! They're dead. They're the *victims*."

I blinked, confused. "They were shot in the middle of an armed robbery while trying to kill police officers. 'Perpetrator' is a simple descriptor."

Kozbar huffed up and leaned in. "Simple-*minded*, perhaps. You have no idea what they went through. Who swayed them away." Kozbar jammed a knife hand at my chest. I parried again, but he paid no notice as he kept jabbing. "Get out. Get out of my mosque."

At home, this would end with an apology (from him), a summons, or Kozbar in cuffs. He would promptly be released from jail by the cowardly DA and the more cowardly mayor, who would be more concerned about having their heads cut off in the middle of Times Square than enforcing the law. But he would at least think twice before pushing around anyone who used words they didn't like. It wasn't a matter of what the end result would be, it was purely a matter of principle.

In this case, I had no recourse that wouldn't escalate the problem. But we couldn't just go quietly. If we let him bully us out of the mosque, he'd be unapproachable later—he'd think he could bully us again. If I thrashed him first, he'd be so hostile later, he'd still be unapproachable—assuming his parishioners didn't drag us out into the street and beat us to death. We needed to have a balance—leave the building on top. There needed to be no mistake that it was *our* choice to leave. It wasn't a matter of ego or pride. It was purely a matter of practicality.

Kozbar jabbed at me again. I parried his right hand with my left, clawed my four fingers around his thumb. I grabbed it with my right hand as well, digging both thumbs into the back of his hand. I twisted the hand to the outside of his body and burst through. It leveraged his body back and down, lest his elbow break.

Kozbar hit the floor with a solid thud. He had martial arts training—he slapped the ground with his free hand to absorb the impact and tucked his chin once he knew he was going to fall—so I followed him down, dropping my knee into his chest to pin him. I stopped short of dropping my full weight on him. He wouldn't have a cracked rib cage, but he'd know I ended up on top.

I pulled back on his arm, twisting it to just short of causing a spiral fracture. It didn't hurt, but it was uncomfortable. "I am *so* sorry about this," I told him unapologetically. "But you shouldn't poke someone who's trained in hand to hand. It can end badly. Reflexes and all. I would like to thank you for your cooperation today, and I look forward to talking to you at a later date. Thanks."

I stood, backed up, gave everyone a friendly wave, and pushed on the doors with my hip so I could keep an eye on all of them as we left.

"Keep walking calmly," I said to Pearson as the doors closed.

We made it a block away before we allowed ourselves to relax. Pearson gave me a sidelong look. "Wasn't that just a tad vengeful for a wonder worker?"

I rolled my eyes. One of the many things I disliked about having my secret out was how other people decided to evaluate my actions. "That would require I be angry. At most, he was annoying. I went through worse abuse as a rookie. It was a purely practical calculation."

Pearson's eyes widened, and his brows shot up. "Really? You didn't even feel a little good about it?"

I shook my head. "Nope. It's not personal for me. If this Soul Stone is a supernatural object that can cause problems, it needs to be back under lock and key. If it's just a fancy rock that someone's using to inspire problems, then we need to get it back."

I stopped in the middle of the sidewalk and frowned. I put my back up against the wall of the nearest building to avoid blocking traffic and looked up. The sky had gotten even darker since we had been in the mosque. I looked at my watch. "Is it always this dark around here at *noon*? Is my watch off?"

Pearson frowned, checked his watch, checked the sky, and said, "Now that you mention it? No. Not really."

The next sensation I had could best be described as a *ping*. Almost like someone had lightly flicked me in the right side of the head, just above my ears. I blinked. The next *ping* flicked against me slightly harder. I looked right. The next *ping* came right between my eyes, but there was no physical source for the sensation.

The next *ping* came both between my eyes, as well as to my left, at ten o'clock.

Those two points had only one thing in common. They were young Muslims ... both wearing long, matching raincoats. Four of them at each point.

It is a common trope that when people lose one sense, their other senses become heightened. Apparently, when I prayed that my sense of smell for evil to be taken away so I could endure the stench of London, I had gotten another sense. Some wonder workers had telepathy in the confessional. I guessed this was going to be as close as I got.

"Get ready, Father," I said *sotto voce*.

Pearson didn't even look down from the dimming sky. "Understood," he said, just as quietly.

I strode back the way we came, taking long steps. The group of Arabs stopped suddenly. Three of them were smart enough to break off from the group, leaving only one man behind.

I smiled at the lone tracker and raised my hand, offering it. "Hello. I'm Thomas Nolan."

Bewildered and uncertain, the tracker raised his hand. "Pleased to—"

I promptly kicked him in the balls. For good measure, when he bent over I dropped a hammer fist on the back of his head, where it meets the spine. He crashed to the sidewalk, catching himself as he fell. He tried to get up. I kicked him in the side of the head. He stopped moving, unconscious.

No. It wasn't a fair fight. But I'm from New York City. As far as we can tell, Marquis of Queensbury is a Ben and Jerry's flavor.

I dropped to a crouch and rolled him over. I quickly frisked him. He had a bottle of acid, which seemed standard at this point, and a machete.

I nearly laughed. *So much for their knife control.* If we were lucky, that meant our pursuers had only melee weapons. If that was the case, we were fine.

Then the automatic rifle fire opened up. *So much for gun control.*

I darted away from the street to brace up against a car wheel for cover.

Pearson looked at me like the world had gone sideways. "Friends of yours?"

I shook my head. "They're new to me. At least, we have some cover, right?"

Then, down the street, back from where we came, cars exploded. I jerked and scrambled away from the explosions. "Down the street!"

What? Did they issue grenade control, too?

Pearson reached for me. I was certain I knew what he was going to say. They were herding us. That was obvious. But there was no other way for us to avoid being blown up.

Then a thick laser beam cut through the cars at the other end of the block like a hot knife through butter. The car exploded at the other end, the gas tank obviously ruptured.

Between the laser at one end and the exploding cars at the other end, there was only one solution. I reached over and grabbed Pearson around the waist. "Hold on."

Levitation, please Lord. We need some levitation—

We shot up four floors in a split second. We came down hard on the roof, but I didn't mind. I pushed to my feet, then yanked Pearson along with me. We crept over to the edge of the roof and looked down. There were a collection of shooters. Two of them had AK-47s. They were spraying without even looking.

Then there were the special ones.

One had a sword ... I wasn't all that surprised. It was curved backwards, a slashing weapon made for horseback. It wasn't that surprising.

Another one used a simple handgun. He aimed for a car, fired, and the car exploded.

The other one fired lasers out of his eyes, slowly sweeping the block, mowing down anything in his way.

Because of course, that's how my luck runs.

Normal people would have decided to take this opportunity to run. It would have been the sensible thing to do. We were out of the line of fire. Any civilians down there were either dead already or running away. We could have left that minute. The armed (and probably armored) London cops would then show up, and they could handle them...

And how many will die in the meantime?

I looked at Pearson. "I've got to stop them before some London cop walks into this without knowing what they're up against. You good here?"

Pearson looked at me, then narrowed his eyes. "Bollocks you're not leaving me here. Fly us back down, and we'll have a right set-to with those thugs. My title is combat exorcist, not retreating Jesuit."

I smiled. I grabbed Pearson again. We took off, and I dropped Pearson on the sidewalk around the corner. I levitated up and over the buildings and came down at the other end of the block, again, around the corner. We had perfect flanking positions right behind them. The automatic weapons chattered deafeningly, and the explosions blotted them out every so often.

I charged in during a lull in the gunfire. I took five large running steps and leaped for the shooter. My left arm slammed against the stock of the AK-47 while my right elbow crashed into the shooter's ear. His head rocked to the side. I swept the rifle up in my hands and slammed the butt of the gun into his face. I slammed his head against the brickwork of a building. I pushed past him, rifle in hand. Oh, cool, it had a bayonet at the end.

I worked the action to check how many rounds were left... The slide was locked open.

It was empty. I flinched. Ahead of me was one of the attackers. His eyes glowed from within, blotting out the pupils, irises, and whites of the eyes.

I guess this is source of the laser beams.

He was ten feet away. I had an empty gun. He had laser eyes. I dove to one side and hurled the AK-47 at him. I had aimed for his chest. Instead, the bayonet slammed into his right leg. He screamed and looked down at his leg at the same moment that his eyes ignited. He didn't blow his own leg off but fired into the sidewalk, reducing it to slag. The recoil of shooting something that close propelled him off the sidewalk and into the side of a building. I sprung to my feet, swept up the rifle, and smashed it into the side of his head. As I intended, I broke the orbital socket, making it compress against the right eye. As a bonus, I broke the nose so it was at right angles to his face.

Laser Eyes laughed. He grabbed the rifle in mid-swing, he focused his brilliant gaze on me. I shoved off of the rifle and dove away from him.

His eyes fired off a beam of energy... which immediately detonated against the broken orbital bone and the disjointed nose.

The resulting explosion gave new meaning to "smoke coming out of his ears." Thankfully, the lasers cauterized the wound, leaving black smoldering holes where his eyes, ears, and jaw used to be.

The light show had caught the attention of Laser Eyes' colleagues. They turned to me.

At the other end of the block, Father Pearson darted around the corner with a loose brick. He slammed it against the first gunman's head. Pearson took the AK and clubbed that gunman down. This caught the attention of the next nearest gunman to him. That was another rifleman and the man with the handgun that fired exploding bullets. Hand Canon stepped back from the car he'd been using as a platform to fire from so he wouldn't shoot his buddy with the AK-47.

Pearson noted the unwanted attention and dove over the hood of the car in front of him, coming down the other side. He darted down the line of parked cars as they exploded. Pearson sped past the car the rifleman had used for cover. He dropped to the street, aimed for the man's ankles, and fired a burst. The bullets tore up his ankles, and he dropped over. Pearson pushed to his feet and burst forward. He came up as Hand Canon bent over to take a look down between the two cars.

Pearson smacked the handgun to one side, stabbed the muzzle of the AK-47 next to the man's ear, and pulled the trigger. The sound blew out his ear, and Pearson disarmed him and clubbed him with the rifle.

Meanwhile, I squared off against three others. Two with AKs, and the third with a sword.

I stood with my hands spread, but at the ready, in a passive stance. "I offer you reconciliation with God and mercy from me if you give up now."

The swordsman smiled. He looked over his shoulder and said, "Take care of the other one."

I picked up the AK again. It wasn't much against a sword, but it had a point. "You don't want to do this."

Swordsman smiled. "I want to do nothing else, infidel."

Then, his sword began to glow. It was bright white and red. In fact, it looked ...

A lightsaber? Are you kidding me?

Swordsman hefted it in a two-handed grip, over his head, and charged me.

I charged him.

As his blade came down, I thrust the AK at his wrists. I met the blow at his wrists with the stock of the rifle, then followed through with a headbutt to his face. He staggered back, then brought the sword down and around, like a baseball swing. I didn't let the swing pass his hips before I slammed the rifle down on his arms. The impact didn't jar the sword from his grip, but it sent him off balance and staggering into a parked car.

The blade sank through the car like it wasn't even there, leaving a burning, melting scar in the engine block. I rammed into him, pinning him to the car.

Then, as the two riflemen approached Pearson, he popped out of concealment and fired a bullet several feet behind and between them.

The resulting explosion knocked the riflemen off their feet. It blew me off of Swordsman and slammed me against the ground. I tried to get up, but my hands and feet met resistance.

I looked down and had to take a beat to process what I saw.

The shadows had crawled up from the sidewalk and slithered around my wrists and ankles like tentacles. For a moment, I thought I had hit my head. Maybe I had been jostled through the time zones too often.

Then the shadows pulled at my arms, forcing them apart, spreading them. I pulled at them, but I might as well pull on chains for all the good it did. They didn't even slow as they pinned me, spread eagle.

Swordsman recovered from the explosion. He saw my predicament and didn't question it. He smiled as he raised his glowing blade over his head. "*Insh'Allah*, infidel."

Father Pearson grabbed his sword hand by the wrist and jammed the pistol into the back of Swordsman's head. "*Deus vult,* heretic. Drop it before I see what this thing does to the human skull at point-blank range."

Swordsman hesitated a moment. "You wouldn't dare. You don't have the moral character we do to die like that."

Pearson tightened his grip and said, "My soul is prepared. How's yours?"

The sword stopped glowing and dropped to the concrete. Pearson smacked him on the side of the head with the pistol to drop him. Swordsman fell to one side. Without Swordsman there, the shadows let me go. I scrambled away from the pavement, a little freaked out. The entire sidewalk was in the shade from awnings, buildings, statues. If any one of them could come alive at any moment ...

This might be harder than I thought.

Pearson helped me to my feet. He had picked up the sword in one hand and still held the pistol. He held the sword upside down. It had a guard over the grip you might see on a pirate cutlass. In the pommel, there was a small fleck. It was perfectly square, and shiny, almost like a piece of oversized glitter. It was perhaps a millimeter squared. There was a matching flake in the pistol grip.

"I checked the bullets," Pearson added. "There's nothing special about them either."

I frowned as I took out my cell phone. I took photos of each and emailed them to myself. I went over to the remains of Laser Eyes to see if I could see anything in what was left of his head.

And there it was, in what some refer to as the third eye, right over the bridge of the nose—another shiny black flake.

I took more pictures. "What did you say that Soul Stone was made of?"

Pearson nodded. "Obsidian."

"And what do these look like to you?"

"The same."

"I figured. I—" I kept taking photos as the flake in the skull of Laser Eyes flashed. It was as though someone flicked a match and it immediately went out. The flakes in the sword and the pistol also flashed out of existence, barely leaving burn marks.

And, of course, at that moment, the police arrived.

7

JURISDICTIONAL CONFLICTS

A aron Shaw was not my idea of Scotland Yard detective. I've met a few. While there is some pomposity that I usually associate with the FBI, he was scruffier than any Scotland Yard officer that I'd ever encountered. He was a little shorter than I was and fairly sturdy, mostly martial arts with a touch of weight lifting. If he couldn't do a five-minute mile, it wasn't that long ago that he could. His brown hair was short-cropped, almost military. But he had a five o'clock shadow and growing. His tan spoke of a career out of town. Somewhere equatorial, perhaps. For some reason, India and Australia came to mind.

Despite the white stonework of the "neo-classical" design of the building from the early 1940s, the inside looked more like a modern office building. The desks were new, fixed with the latest in ports for wires to go through. The technology was relatively up to date, though I wouldn't want to ask about the software. But it still had to be better than whatever I was running at my police station PC. Despite the technology, the piles of paperwork and the photos of suspects clearly denoted this as a police station.

Shaw's office was modern, meaning it was a glass box with a

window. There were fewer signs of this being a police officer's desk, but I could still see it.

Shaw stared at my badge for far, far too long. "New York, huh?" he said, his voice like a growl. He rolled his ice blue eyes as he hurled it back at me. "You people are all alike. You come to our country, cause trouble, and don't even offer us the courtesy of a check-in."

I caught the badge case without thinking about it. I didn't take my eyes off of him as I slid it away. "Don't take it personally. New York does this to whatever country it feels like. Though to be perfectly frank, I didn't think my investigation would tread on anyone's toes until the bullets flew." I shrugged, a model of innocence. "I didn't think that they allowed guns in London."

As we all know, a model is what one gets when one cannot get the real thing.

Shaw's eyes narrowed, and my blood froze. I couldn't tell if it was supernatural, or just him.

Shaw leaned forward. "I want you to understand me, *Mister* Nolan," Shaw growled. "We don't need American cowboys running around, starting fights and harassing a respected community leader like Imam Kozbar."

I barked a laugh. It was involuntary, honest. "His communicants tried to kill me."

Shaw smirked. "And?"

I nodded slowly. It only then dawned on me that this wasn't going to end well, no matter how it was spun. There was no brotherhood of blue in this office. "Is self-defense illegal around here?"

"It is when you poke the bear."

I arched my brows, wondering if he had just admitted to something. Because that implication was fairly obvious. "Did Kozbar really sic gunmen on me?"

"Of *course* not!" Shaw scoffed. "You obviously upset someone in his mosque, who felt threatened enough to go after you on a crowded street."

I nodded slowly, thinking over everything I had heard since I arrived. "Tell me, is that official police policy? The mayor? Or your own personal thoughts on the matter?"

Shaw tried far too hard to play cat with the canary. I knew because I played that part myself at times. "I'm sure that we treat Kozbar as delicately as you would treat a Cardinal."

I laughed. "I have to make sure someone tells the Cardinal that he can get away with armed men in the street."

Shaw grunted and threw his hands in the air. "It doesn't matter. You're nicked, son. And I have control over you and how the rest of your day is going to go."

"On what charge?"

Shaw grinned. "Disturbing the peace. Possession of a firearm."

It was my turn to scoff dismissively. "It was one of theirs, and they were shooting at me."

"Prove it."

"Don't you have CCTV all over this city?"

Shaw smiled evilly. It must be the smile of every local cop who had the opportunity to throw an interloper—from Fed to private investigator—into jail. "They've been down in Whitechapel for the better part of the day. So terribly sorry for the inconvenience."

Shaw wasn't sorry.

I felt aggravated with myself. It was standard for me to wear a police camera on the job. Not detectives, me. Mainly because my life was too strange to verify without documented evidence. But I had left that behind me when I left New York.

"Into the cells with you. Constable!" he barked. A young man in a white shirt and black vest came in. "Take Mister Nolan here to the cells. Book him on disturbing the peace, harassment of a public official. And be sure to put him into the same cell with his friends from the mosque."

Aw crap.

After I had been booked, I had been pushed into a holding cell. It was okay. It would have been comfortable enough for seven people, if six of them hadn't been people who I had just gotten into a fist fight with in the middle of the street. They turned at my approach and stood as the door opened. I waited for the door to click shut.

I leaned up against the bars of the cell. I put my hands behind me and smiled at the men who had tried to kill me. "Hello. My name is Thomas Nolan. Though you already know that, don't you?"

Despite having various and sundry band-aids and patches for all of the damage we gave them, all of them closed in.

I took a deep breath and let it out slowly. *Lord God almighty, I will take any beating you deem that I should receive. The Lord giveth, the Lord taketh away, blessed be the Name of the Lord. But if You don't mind, I'm going to fight back.*

"I want to know where you got your weapons today." I glanced at the ones who had been using AK-47s. "And I don't mean the rifles. The sword and the handgun were modified with obsidian. I don't think it was supposed to be ornamental. Where did it come from?"

Swordsman smiled at me. He was missing teeth. I don't think I'd contributed to them. "Allah HIMSELF gave them to us. Just as Allah has given us *you.*"

Funny, Shaw doesn't look like Allah. "What *human* hand gave them to you?"

Swordsman laughed. "Wouldn't you like to know?"

I blinked. "Yes. That's why I'm asking."

Swordsman spread his hands wide. "You now belong to us to do with as we wish. Allah be praised. Allah! Send us your aid! Allah! Drag this infidel into the darkness! Where he may suffer and die!"

I felt the shadows move around me, touching me, slight wisps along my skin. Ready to attack like they did before. *That's it!*

I reached forward, grabbed Swordsman by the shirt front, and pulled him towards me. I twisted, slamming him face first into the bars. I twisted back the other way, hurling him into one of his compatriots. I whirled and hammer-fisted another of my cell buddies. I pounded right into the head wound where Pearson had smashed him with a rock. He crumpled. I leaped over him and drove into Hand Gun. I plowed into him, slamming him against attacker number five, and smashed them both into a wall. I grabbed the head of Hand Gun, pulled him towards me, and slammed his skull into the nose of the man behind him. After three smacks with the organic bowling ball we call the human head, Hand Gun was dazed, and his friend had passed out.

I stepped back with my right foot and hurled Hand Gun's head with my body weight. Since that was his center of balance, the rest of his body went with him.

I looked over the men in the cell. Only one was still standing. He had scrambled out from underneath Swordsman.

God, thank You for ... oh, just thank You. I'll get specific later.

I stalked towards the last man standing. He was one of the AK-47 users. "Now look. I have spent years on the NYPD without ever—not once—even *considering* beating a suspect. If you want me to start now, you have only to throw a punch at me. We can continue the interrogation when you're on your back."

He raised his hands in surrender. "I don't know. I was given a rifle."

I rocked my head as I backed him up against the bars. "Elaborate."

"We were given rifles and sent out after you. The other three met up with us as we were coming to get you."

The "other three" must have been Hand Gun, Swordsman, and Laser Eyes. "You've never seen them before?"

He shook his head. "No. No, of course not."

"Define *of course*. Why not?"

"I—"

"Oi! What's going on here!"

I sighed and stepped back from the last man standing. One of the cops came in. "What the Hell happened here?"

I shrugged. "Inspector Shaw threw me in with the people who tried to kill me. You'll have to ask him."

The cop narrowed his eyes as he unlocked the door. "Come along. You're out."

I followed the officer right out the front door of the Met. Father Pearson was waiting for me. The cop didn't say anything as he handed me a clear plastic bag with my personal belongings. After I reloaded my pockets, I handed him back the bag. He handed me a receipt to sign, I did, and he walked away without another word.

"Enjoy your stay?" Pearson asked.

I shrugged. "More or less. How did you get out?"

Pearson smiled. "I had a conversation with Inspector Shaw's superiors." He took out his phone. "I had the conversation with Kozbar filmed, as well as the shootout."

I arched a brow. The shootout started, we levitated, and then closed with the shooters. "Not the—"

"No, I waited until we were back on terra firma to start the video up again."

I nodded. The last thing I needed was to have video footage of my abilities.

We walked along for a bit. I hadn't noticed that night had fallen during my stay. I checked my watch. It was only seven in the evening. I checked the sky again. If there were storm clouds overhead, I couldn't tell. The sky was a solid ceiling of black. There were no stars. There was no moon.

"This isn't a good sign," I stated.

"Precisely. Tomorrow, our progress should be faster. Much faster."

I considered his comment. Normally, I would work through the night, especially when things were warming up this hot.

But you have no authority here, Tommy. You're not going to do anything after business hours. Whether you like it or not.

"First food, then hotel."

8

BAD DREAMS

I walked into the hotel lobby tired and achy. I looked forward to a nice, relaxing sleep. Nightmares wouldn't have bothered me that much as long as I could sleep. Fighting my way just to get to mass that morning, plus getting shot at outside of the Mosque and spending hours in lockup and getting into a fist fight there too...

Come to London on a mission from God. Get into more fights than you ever did in New York. Have few to no leads ... except for the one group who tried to kill you. And you can't get to them, either, because they're in lock-up. Tell me again, Lord, what am I doing here?

Never mind. I'm sent on a mission from You. Something will move eventually.

The only real question would have been the next step. There was obviously a connection between the Soul Stone and the Whitechapel mosque. But how would one investigate that without a tactical team? I couldn't even ask Imam Kozbar a few inoffensive questions without starting a fist fight with him. I swore I could have heard him ranting and raving about how much bigotry was involved in even asking questions about Muslims shooting up the British Museum or the street outside. Not to mention that they were beaten in custody by—

I stopped and turned to the lobby television. Kozbar was on the screen, holding a press conference. The Imam mentioned his dead parishioners at the Museum and decried the racism behind their "assassination." Kozbar railed against the "increasing assaults on Muslims in London," citing assault with acid, torture by breaking fingers, even an attack on Kozbar himself.

Then I realized that all of those "racist attacks" after the museum referred to me.

I sighed and kept trudging on through the dark passages of the hotel. I watched as the Imam continued in the same vein for several minutes. And then, London's mayor joined up and said the same thing. I weathered this onslaught of rewriting history, waiting to hear my name, or "American" or "New York Detective." Thankfully, none of these words were uttered. I felt like it was a miracle that no one showed my photo.

It felt like the story of my life, where the moral of the story was that no good deed goes unpunished. Stop an abortionist turned serial killer? I was called a racist and a bigot for beating up on a "doctor for providing a service." Shoot to wound? Be accused of torture. And that was only the first problem a year ago. Those were only the people who weren't actively trying to kill me.

Between being exhausted and once more getting crucified in the media, I skulked off down the dark hallways of the hotel.

If this wasn't the one thing to cause an overwhelming urge to call home, nothing was. Yes, I know that I haven't been left alone at all since I left New York. And yes, I had been separated from my family before, and for longer periods. But all I really needed was to hear Mariel's voice. Besides, it felt more natural to call home than to call Father Pearson and discuss this most recent kick in the guts.

I pulled out my phone and called home. I would send the Vatican a bill.

The phone picked up almost immediately. I blinked, surprised. "Mariel? Jeremy?"

"Hello?" my wife asked clearly through the phone. "Who's this?"

I smiled. I couldn't help it. "It's Tommy. How are you?"

"Tommy!" she growled.

I winced and yanked the phone away from my ear. When she picked up, she sounded like my wife. But her voice and her mood had turned on a dime. We'd been through pregnancy hormones before, but this took the cake.

"Mariel?' I asked.

"You! You left us! Go away, Tommy. I'm leaving you."

Then the phone call turned off.

I was left standing in front of the elevator with a glassy stare reminiscent of a stunned ox.

Mariel? My Mariel? Had just left me? How could that have happened? This was the women I had met at the range. She organized the church gun club. She had stayed with me through serial killers, a SWAT team kicking in the front door, a zombie attack on the house, the kidnapping of our son, even her own throat being slit.

I tried calling back. Then I tried again. I spent the next ten minutes alternating between hitting the elevator's call button and hitting redial. The calls did not go through.

How could a few days away turn into her leaving me?

I was so rocked by what just happened, I missed my elevator several times. I absently pressed the button again. I felt numb inside. With a little peace and quiet, I could feel my heart beating, and be aware of my internal organs.

My cell phone alerts went off. My spirits lifted for a moment...

Instead, it was a commercial. I blinked, confused, as the video automatically started playing on my phone. The opening image was possibly the cutest baby marketing could find, smiling and happy, with a white knit watch cap and the brightest blue eyes I had ever seen. The music was the standard mobile chimes of "Lullaby and goodnight," also known as Schubert's Opus 49.

A text box read: "She deserves to be... loved."

More happy smiling toothless baby. More Text: "She deserves to be... wanted."

An even happier baby. "She deserves to be ... a choice. #StandWiththeWHC."

The bottom fell out of my stomach. I felt like throwing up and hurling my phone. Or hurling and throwing my phone. The Women's Health Corps? I had driven a stake into the organization months ago. They were the front for a death cult dedicated to the demon Moloch. Now they were advertising *on the internet*? Why weren't they all in *jail*? They had threatened my family, tried to kill my wife and kidnapped my son, and they were still *around*?

At that moment, I felt so numb, even walking felt like a dream. I had gotten to the door of my hotel room without having any recollection of getting on the elevator or walking the long hallway to my room door. I had already turned the key in the lock.

I pushed the door open into the utter blackness of the room. I took one step inside and froze.

It was *freezing*. It was like someone had left the air conditioning on in the middle of an igloo. It was the emptiness of space wrapped in an iceberg.

I hadn't felt cold this bad since ...

Curran!

Then it hit me. The entire phone call with Mariel suddenly made sense.

The phone call had been interfered with.

The original demon I tangled with had been skilled at disrupting my phone calls. I couldn't get good reception for days. It had dumped endless static onto the phone lines. Why couldn't a more skilled demon take a more nuanced approach to disrupting communications? Remove the static. Edit words. Change the tone of words.

Because demons liked nothing better than grinding people down.

I looked at the alert on my phone. I had been "alerted" to an ad from the Women's Health Corps that was over a year old.

Whatever this was had manipulated me into thinking my wife was leaving me and an archenemy was coming back.

I went from numb to a far more unfamiliar sensation. I was enraged.

"Saint Michael the Archangel, defend us in battle," I snarled. The darkness recoiled from me and slid back along the floor. "Be our protection against the wickedness and snares of the devil. May

God rebuke him we humbly pray; and do Thou, O Prince of the Heavenly Host, by the Power of God, cast into hell Satan and all the evil spirits, who prowl through the world seeking the ruin of souls. Amen."

The shadows on the floor slithered into a corner. It congealed into a lump of darkness on the floor. It slid and bubbled on the rug.

I reached into my back pocket, grabbed my rosary, and hurled it at the mess. The shadows recoiled, flowing around it and backing up the wall. It formed an eerie, man-shaped form on the wall. It spread wings along the wall.

And then the form peeled away from the wall and reached out for me.

I took three steps across the room towards the shadow in the wall and punched the shadow in the ... head.

The shadow recoiled with the punch, sliding back onto the wall.

I jabbed a finger in the shadow's direction. "In the name of Jesus Christ, our Lord and Savior, in the name of Yahweh, Creator of all, I order you back to Hell."

The shadow froze for a moment ... then it threw back its head and laughed. It laughed as it slid away and faded back into the rest of the darkness.

Before I could even utter a *thank you* to God for once more saving my ass, I was hit with a rotten, decaying smell.

And since I had turned off that particular charism, that meant that this was something that anyone in the hotel could smell this.

Which means that whatever this is, is still here. I just dealt with a small part of it...But then again, I smelled evil over the whole city at 20,000 feet...

It took me a beat to consider that it wasn't my room. It wasn't even the hotel.

It was the entire city.

And they were focusing on me, then, in that room.

The room shook. I grabbed my suitcase and hurled it out into the hallway. Then I dove out the door after it and rolled.

...The hallway was dead silent except for the thunderous beating of my heart.

I took my suitcase and went straight down into the lobby. I immediately grabbed the nearest pay phone and called Father Pearson.

"Get me the Hell out of this death trap," I told him. "And start sharpening your combat exorcism skills—you're going to need them."

9

BEING REASONABLE

Father Pearson didn't send a cab for me. Pearson came himself, with a deacon driving the car. A second car pulled up behind him. They were men in black with a military bearing and swarmed into the lobby. They moved past me and didn't even glance my way. Father Pearson came up to me, grabbed my suitcase, and calmly said, "Come along."

We were loaded into the car and pulled away in under a minute.

As we pulled away from the curb, another car came up and replaced us. It was a police car. Aaron Shaw and a squad of cops swept out onto the sidewalk. As we sped away, more police cars swarmed the area.

"Well!" Pearson said, chipper, "that was a fortuitous bit of timing."

I looked at him like he was insane. Then again, going by his job title, after battling the first few possessed, I'd be lucky to hold on to whatever marbles I had. Not to mention that he wasn't the one who had nearly just been devoured by living darkness.

Though the idea that Shaw had just happened to show up after I had nearly been attacked was a strange coincidence. Normally, I would think that Shaw had something to do with demonic forces...

though that could have taken the form of anything from actual demons to political considerations. Either way, Shaw was guided by the forces of darkness.

Along the way, I talked, and Pearson listened. His bright and cheery attitude faded as I went along. Though he did approve of me punching a shadow entity in the face.

"I won't say that the entire city is infested with demons," Pearson finally concluded when I was finished. He slid back in the seat, his hands folded together. "Because I don't want to jump to conclusions. However, I will say that it's demonic in nature. Whatever it is. You may have severed a limb from the beast. Or they're minor demons and part of a larger problem. Either way, this will be annoying."

"That's one word for it."

We made it to the rectory of Westminster Cathedral. Pearson immediately led me to his rooms in the rectory. He moved away for a moment and let me be while he set up a room for me.

I looked around the cell. Pearson's chambers were heavy with books. Books on shelves that went up to the ceiling. The books were from various of authors. Everyone from Knock and Chesterton to John C. Wright, Declan Finn, and L. Jagi Lamplighter. Other titles included *The Rite* and *Tales of an Exorcist*. I grabbed a novel off the shelf and flipped some pages. Strangely enough, Pearson had annotated a vampire novel with comments like "This might work" or even "What does he know and who told him?"

I frowned, put it back, and didn't think that I was going to look at any of the other novels. I preferred my fiction to remain fiction... Though given the life I'd had up to that point, there was no real way to tell the difference. Between the vampire mercenaries, the flaming Balrog drone, the Voodoo Bokor and the warlock mayor, the only difference between my life and an urban fantasy novel seemed to be the decided lack of bisexual group sex with were-furries. I noted that *those* books were unsurprisingly lacking from this collection.

Pearson came back twenty minutes later. I was thirty pages into *War Demons* from a small publisher called Silver Empire. (The annotations in that one included lines like "Look up the demon type" and "Confirm OpSec.")

"Your rooms are made up," Pearson told me.

I nodded. "Oh, thank you." I raised the book and showed it to him. "Your marginalia are interesting."

Pearson's friendly smile dropped. He reached over and took it out of my hand. "We have other editions that are less marked up."

I was surprised. The demeanor shift was sudden. "Too many secrets revealed?"

"No comment," Pearson said flatly. "Now, your room's ready."

The moment I entered the cell, I dialed home.

"Hello?" Jeremy answered.

My entire body sagged. "Hey, kiddo. How are you?"

"Awesome! Did you call earlier? Mommy said we got a call with nothing but static."

I smiled broadly. Not only had the demonic forces that work manipulated the conversation, they didn't even have any of Mariel's words to edit. "Yeah. That was me. Can she talk?"

"Of course, I can," she came on. "How are you, Tommy?"

I smiled as I sat down on the bed with a thud. "I'm ... fine."

"What's wrong, Tommy?"

I forced a smile so she could hear it. "Nothing. Not anymore. Could you... just talk to me? I miss the sound of your voice."

Mariel laughed. "Tommy. You haven't even been gone a week."

"Humor me."

She talked. I listened.

My SLEEP that night was fitful. No surprise. I didn't need horrific visions to chase me in my nightmares. I had lived through too many of them. The shadows that had come after me had inspired bad dreams of Mayor Hoynes sending shadows after me.

I made it to morning mass at six. I rolled out of bed and into mass.

It was a peaceful time, and it relaxed the anxieties of the night before. I was also fully dressed in suit and shirt, overcoat, and left the tie in my suitcase.

After mass, I strolled out of the cathedral and hoped to get a few minutes of air before breakfast. I considered stopping in the McDonald's on the corner, but it struck me as moronic to eat something abroad that I could have anywhere back home.

However, before I could get anywhere, Dame Polly Toynbee and Lord Newby Fowler were waiting for me.

The two aristocrats stood outside the front doors looking disdainfully at the congregation as they walked past. Fowler was in full undertaker dress—black suit, tie, white shirt—carrying an umbrella and wearing a bowler hat. Dame Toynbee was in dark purple, hanging on his left arm, along with his umbrella.

Lord Fowler smiled broadly. "Good morning, Officer Nolan! Might we interest you in a walk around the block? We wanted to see how you were doing this morning, and we missed you at your hotel."

Fowler offered me his hand. I took it cautiously. I generally disliked the feeling that came off these two. They felt like living store mannequins—perfectly and unnaturally poised like they were a window display set that had come to life. I couldn't tell if that was the natural artifice that came with their station and upbringing, or public relations, or if they were concealing something. Either way, it didn't fit comfortably with the blunt, straightforward people I genuinely dealt with.

Hell. Even the mayor and the WHC were gracious enough to show their disdain for me before they tried to murder me.

"I have no complaints," I told him. And I didn't. Complaining about my job was counterproductive.

Fowler slowly tilted his head. "Indeed? I think you're being disingenuous with us, Officer. You changed hotels. Surely there was something to complain about."

I shrugged. He had a point that I didn't think about. I had been so busy blotting last night out of my brain, I had problems thinking about the hotel as having a problem... that was like complaining that a house was a little drafty in the middle of a hurricane.

I gestured to the cathedral. "This was more convenient. Closer to my assistant, and it's easier for me to get to mass in the morning."

Fowler and Toynbee exchanged a sudden concerned glance between them. Fowler gestured behind him so we could start walking away from the cathedral. He did it in such a conspiratorial manner that it was like he thought the cathedral could overhear his conversation.

"We didn't want to bring this up the other day," Fowler began, "but we are concerned about your assigned researcher in this manner."

I arched a brow. "Really?"

"Indeed," Dame Toynbee said. "Oh, dear me, and is it really safe being in this Church? Jesuits can be so very sinister, you know."

We walked along for three paces before I could answer, "Actually, I think he's Opus Dei."

Fowler laughed. It was a rich, clear sound. "Doesn't that even make it worse? All those radicals. It can't be healthy."

I tried not to roll my eyes. Ever since those stupid anti-Christian propaganda novels masquerading as thrillers were forced down the throat of the public, I'd heard all sorts of odd and ignorant conspiracy theories about my entire faith.

"Opus Dei is actually a lay movement," I explained calmly. "Maybe 2% of the entire organization is ordained."

Fowler rolled his eyes. "Oh, please. The entire organization is freakish and unreal. After all, no sex before marriage? Restraining sexual urges? Everyone has sex. It's unnatural to show that sort of restraint."

I didn't feel like explaining to them that I made certain to keep it zipped until Mariel and I were married. I also didn't see what the point of the conversation was. Had they come to ask after me, dig for information, or lecture me?

"You'd be surprised," I said neutrally. I found it usually worked to keep my mouth shut. Some people had problems with silence and rushed to fill the vacuum with sound.

"Oh please. Look at all those rubes stumbling around in their superstitious fog. I can tell you're not like them, Nolan. You can handle the truth. That nothing exists apart from physical matter and energy? We all know that there's no God, right? Going to mass must just be good cover while you're working with a priest."

Fowler said it so jovially, I could only conclude that he believed it. I was tempted to tell him my brother was a priest, just to see what his reaction would be like, but that would be mean. Entertaining, but mean. The last time I heard someone so self-righteous about there being nothing out there was when I had run into the most evangelical faith I knew.

"I presume you're both atheists?" I asked.

Fowler laughed. "Of course we are. We are educated, after all."

Toynbee smiled at me and added, "It is so nice to find another educated man. They're the only ones to talk to. Better than workmen. They seem to all think that news is all propaganda and skips the leading articles. A workman buys a paper for football results and little paragraphs about girls falling out of windows and corpses found in flats."

Fowler shook his head and sighed. "True. They are a problem. We will have to recondition him eventually. But the educated public, the people who read the high-brow weeklies, don't need reconditioning. They're all right already. They'll believe whatever the papers print, after all."

I nodded slowly. The bad vibrations I got off of them now could have vibrated me right out of my shoes. "I presume you own one or two of them."

"Of course. It's the only way to get the good word out to the great heart of the British public. It's the only way to make it hear what we want. Like the re-education of the maladjusted, or getting the dear little kiddies free education in experimental schools."

I made the mistake of asking, "Is that for everyone or specific kids?"

"Oh, just the religious," Toynbee chirped.

Fowler nodded. "We have to get rid of the detritus *somehow*."

Toynbee smiled broadly. "Personally, I think we're *very* close to making religious households deemed as abusive to children."

I nodded very slowly, like I would with any emotionally disturbed person holding me at knifepoint. "Indeed. I hope it all ends well," I said, meaning that I hoped they had a strong and sudden conversation with the cosmic baseball bat that was once used on the road to Damascus. "Good luck with the Imams," I said sarcastically. "Kozbar especially."

I could only imagine what Kozbar would do with Fowler and Toynbee. I had only asked a few questions and nearly received a beating. Declare faith abusive? I'd expect a war first.

Fowler dismissed my concern with a wave of his hand. "Oh, Islam isn't the problem. Christians are far more insidious."

I missed a step and nearly stumbled at that outlandish statement. "Then you should tell the head of the Church of England. That is still the King, isn't it?"

Fowler gave me a pitying look. "Really, now? That isn't Christianity. It's pragmatic."

I nodded slowly, letting him think I believed his point. The more cynical (cough, Thomas Hobbes, cough) have suggested that the Anglican church was a great idea to keep around, because the *idea* of God in Heaven was worth more than a police officer on every corner. Then again, that also required the belief that humans were so lousy that the world would turn into *Lord of the Flies* if there wasn't the boogeyman called God in the cosmic closet. I have made too many close acquaintances among the prison population to believe that.

But right now, I needed the hell away from these two. Frankly, I had conversations that made more sense with my late friend Erin, who was a pagan. At least with her, we could agree that there was more to life than what we could see.

"Is atheism your main cause?" I asked.

"In our spare time," Toynbee answered.

Fowler shrugged. "Though there's so little free time, in between the newspaper, being the curators of the museum, and manufacturing and materials."

I nodded slowly and made it a point to look them up later. "Pardon me, but I should be getting back on the case of the Soul Stone. By the way, how did you find me?"

Fowler smiled. "We called the rectory. They told us where to find you."

10

CUI BONO?

I got away from Lord Fowler and Dame Toynbee. It took everything I had not to break into a run and get away from their "reasonable" conversation. They wanted to talk to me about cosmology when we couldn't even agree on the nature of the cosmos. It felt like talking to someone who needed tinfoil to keep out the radio signals.

As I made it back to the cathedral, Father Pearson was already on the steps of the church, waiting for me. He was still in full vestments. He gave me a curious look, wondering where I was.

"I was just paid a visit by Fowler and Toynbee."

Pearson clasped his hands together and rolled his eyes. "Ah! Yes! Did they decide to give you their standard 'We know you're one of the special ones' routine?"

"They've done this before?" I asked.

He rolled his eyes. "Routinely. They've also bought into the idea that if you believe in evolution, you're just one skip step away from becoming one of the enlightened ones."

I rolled my eyes this time. A little too hard. "Really? Enlightened ones? What? They think they're the Illuminati?"

"Actually, they call themselves the Brights," he said dryly. "No, I'm not joking."

I sighed as I walked back into the church. "I didn't know it was as screwed up over here as it is back home."

"Maybe more," he replied.

Pearson led the way into the rectory. He went over to the hat rack with all of the hangers for the multiple parts of his vestments and started to dismantle his assortment. "What shall we do today? Go back to Whitechapel?"

Even the casual calm, non-threatening way that Pearson said that made me shiver ... mostly because of the history of the area. I had seen several brochures for the "Jack the Ripper Walking Tour."

I preferred the Vlad the Impaler walks in Transylvania.

"It's a bit of a tossup," I answered him, thinking out loud. "Sure, we were attacked by Muslims, but why? Do we assume they're working for Kozbar? There are seven thousand people in his parish. Do we assume that he's so well informed that people can't slip past him without him knowing? I wouldn't. I don't think my pastor could identify half the congregation by name. He probably can't even recognize the other half by face."

Pearson hung up the green top piece of the vestments. He smoothed it down. "I wouldn't place bets one way or another, to be honest. Just because he's an Imam doesn't necessarily make him evil."

I sat down while he changed. "Here's another problem. What about the way the plan was pulled off? There are times where thugs aren't the smartest people on the planet. But it seemed a little too obvious where we should be looking. Isn't it? Is it just me?"

Pearson shook his head with a thoughtful frown but was more focused on peeling off the second layer of his vestments than looking at me. "That works both ways. It could be a diversion from somebody else, someone who hired a few Whitechapel folks to distract from who organized it. Or it could be a way of keeping the police from investigating it—whether on orders from the mayor or out of a sense that they'll be a riot if they investigated anyone within an arm swing of Kozbar."

I nodded slowly. "Or both."

Pearson sighed as he hung up the white cloth. "Exactly. It could be exactly what it appears to be *and* used to distract us. The question is, distract us from what?"

I didn't say anything for a moment. I waited for Pearson to hang up the last of his vestments and sit.

"Here's the best question to ask: who benefits? From any of this? What about the Fowlers? Was there any insurance on the Stone? They're creepy enough."

Pearson shook his head. "Not that I know of. Why would they steal their own stone? Why not just take it?"

"Good point. And besides, they're atheists. They wouldn't believe in the legend of the rock. Can the Soul Stone be sold? What's it worth? What can anyone get out of an item that's so blatant and visible that it has to be broken up?"

"And it can't even be broken up."

I blinked. "Repeat that."

Pearson shrugged. "It can't be broken up. They tried back at the museum so they could date it. Didn't work." He leaned back in the chair and tilted it back a little bit. "As to the worth? Well, if we go by the legend of the stone, it could be damn near anything."

I frowned. "Tell me the whole thing."

Pearson took a breath and thought it over. "Keep in mind, much of what we know comes from the notes found in one of Saddam Hussein's palaces. He had taken it from Gamal Nasser of Egypt. Don't even ask what the deal was, there were no notes about it. But Nasser wanted it far away from him. As I mentioned before, the legend that came with the Soul Stone is that it was handed to the first dynasty Pharaoh by Anubis himself."

It took me a quick moment to remember Anubis as the Egyptian god of the dead. "I don't think I'd want to keep that gift if I could avoid it."

Pearson shrugged. "Anubis was considered relatively benevolent as far as gods go. First, he was the protector of graves and lord of the underworld, and when Osiris replaced him, Anubis became the embalmer, or guide for souls to the afterlife. He also had some authority over divination. So that itself wasn't a warning sign. According to the Iraqis, the Soul Stone absorbs the misery and suffering of a city, and when it is fully charged, it becomes a weapon."

I blinked. It wasn't the most outrageous story I'd heard, but it ranked up there. I had little problem with the idea of demons—that idea was eternal. I had no problem with someone exchanging his soul for power—again, that was a tale as old as fairy stories. But an evil rock?

But then again, as Pearson told me when this all began, the Soul Stone had been in a torture chamber in one of Saddam's palaces. "Considering where you found it, you figure that Saddam believed this crap?"

"I'd lay money on it."

I tried to dredge up what little I could remember about the former dictator of Iraq. "But wasn't Saddam crazy?"

Pearson arched a brow. "Excuse me, weren't you the one being attacked by shadows? Why *not* believe this?"

I laughed. "True enough." I shook my head, thinking this over. I had gone from demonic people to demonic artifacts. "Why does my life seem to just get stranger? And this insanity *started* when a demonic serial killer came for my family." I readjusted in my seat, straightening up. "Anyway, evil rock. Fine. But if they couldn't cut the stone at the museum, how did they put stone flakes in their weapons? Or the skin?"

"And the stone couldn't be cut or chipped in the legends. If the Soul Stone is truly everything they say it is, it makes no sense."

Pearson frowned. I frowned.

Then I shrugged. "If it's everything they say it is, then the only thing that could damage the stone would be the stone itself, right?"

Pearson paused, blinked, cocked his head, and said, "Maybe. May … be. Which means that they didn't *cut* pieces off of it, but they *willed* them off. Sheer force of will, directing the stone to take off pieces of itself."

I was about to compliment Pearson on the idea when there came a faint booming sound.

Boom.

Boom.

Boom boom boom.

And it repeated.

I looked at Pearson. "Are you expecting anyone?"

Pearson shook his head. "Not now. I locked up behind us since we'd be out of here in a few minutes, and everyone else is out."

I shrugged. "Should we go out the side?"

We went out the back of the church and circled around the buildings in the front. He came out on the street and walked along the curb. Coming at the plaza from the back, we found a sight that I wish I could have said surprised me. A crowd of forty angry people.

Pearson was even more cynical. "Oh look. A crowd of angry Muslims. I wonder if they've come to file a complaint about a Hagar the Horrible comic strip."

I looked at him and smiled. He said, "What?"

"No. It's just that you reminded me of my partner there for a moment."

Pearson shrugged and looked back to the mob banging on the door of the Cathedral. There were several Molotov cocktails. They threw rocks at the front door. The next step would be the windows.

Pearson stepped forward. In a loud, booming voice that hinted at time in the military, barked, "Can I help you, gentlemen?"

The mob turned towards us. The front ranks came up from the doors to approach us.

The bottom fell out of my stomach. In the front ranks were people I knew. One was from The Museum, whose fingers I had broken. One had a face scarred with acid, from the Cathedral attack of yesterday morning.

And behind them? Swordsman, Hand Gun, and several of the riflemen from yesterday afternoon, after the visit to the mosque in Whitechapel.

Better and better. I don't even need to guess what they're here for.

Acid Face pointed at me. "That's him! Get him!"

One of the men with him raised his hands. Lightning crackled between his fingers. Then he hurled it at us.

11

LAST MAN STANDING

I shoved Pearson to one side as I dove forward, rolling under the lightning bolt. If this guy was like Laser Eyes from yesterday, then it would work best to get closer to him, not farther away. If I could engage him close to the crowd, he couldn't use his powers without hurting one of the friends who came with him.

I came out of the roll, bounding to my feet...

Unfortunately, I kept going *up*. It wasn't levitation this time, but a gust of wind that blew me off the ground. I slapped the ground and rolled backwards, over my shoulder and back on my feet.

Unfortunately, that meant that the crowd saw it and closed. And one flank swarmed over Father Pearson first.

My adrenaline kicked in, and I darted for Pearson.

A man stopped in front of me, swinging a knife. The crowd kept a wide berth of the knife, lest they get cut with it. I backpedaled, letting the swipe go past my face. On the backhand, I shot into it, meeting his arm with the backs of my forearms. I twisted my hands around and hooked down with my fingers, grabbing the wrist and forearm of the knife wielder. Without any fanfare, I slammed the man's own knife, still held in his grip, right into his throat.

I wrapped my right hand around the hand holding the knife,

yanked on the fist, without even leaving my fingerprints on it. I then jammed it into his own stomach. I twisted him around and shoved him at some of his own friends.

I went for Pearson.

Pearson, meanwhile, had been jumped on by a man wielding rebar. Pearson wheeled back, out of the way of the swing, and pressed in before the attacker's arm could come back around. He checked the offending arm with his left and drove an elbow into his attacker's throat. Pearson grabbed the rebar out of his attacker's hand and backhanded it into the face of the next attacker in line. He swung around with a strike to the first attacker's face, dropping both of them. The next piece of rebar came in an overhead swing. With a two-handed grip, Pearson blocked with his rebar and stomped on the man's knee, dislocating it. The man crumpled.

Pearson saw me coming and tossed me the second piece of rebar. I leaped to grab it.

A gust of wind sent the rebar in one direction, and me in another. I didn't see where the rebar ended up, but I landed on the curb, and rolled into the street, in front of an oncoming bus.

I scrambled to the sidewalk. A bus nearly clipped me. I made it to my feet.

Right in front of me were two men, only six feet in front of me. One was the lightning thrower. The other was the man I had stabbed with his own knife. Everyone else gave them room to work – no one wanted to get hit by a stray bolt of lightning.

I only just noticed the faint glint of black obsidian embedded in both of their foreheads.

The man with lightning fingers said, "I am Bariq."

The man who should be dead waved. "Shifa."

Bariq grinned. "Die."

I ducked down and drove forward, underneath the lightning again. I slammed my shoulder into Bariq's right shin while cupping my hands behind his ankle. This forced him backwards, and I bowled him over. I stayed on my feet, with my hold still on his leg. I twisted him over and forced him on his face to keep from being struck with lightning. I straightened and back-fisted Shifa in the side of the neck. He went down, but it wouldn't keep him down forever.

I stomped on Bariq's kidney since I didn't want him popping up after me again any time soon.

Pearson ran up to me, grabbed my arm, and yanked me along after him, running down the street. The wind picked up. I had a sudden bad feeling about all of the strange wind patterns. I looked up.

There he was, a chubby Arab with an outlandish head covering that looked more like a Sikh Turban than anything else, with a long gray beard that came down to the belt covering his large gut. And he was walking on air. I could see the faint outline of a tornado underneath him.

Great. I'm fighting Jihadi X-Men. I've already met Storm and Wolverine. I guess I killed Cyclops yesterday.

It was even worse when the clouds gathered, turning a murky morning pitch black.

As we ran, a young couple with begging signs looked around them in confusion as everyone started clearing the streets.

I grabbed the arm of one. Pearson grabbed the other. We pulled them along with us as we headed for the train station. We charged down the stairs, the mob hot on our heels. But since we didn't have to fight the wind in the train station, we moved faster. Once we were certain that our homeless friends knew to break off down another hallway, we moved even faster. We sprinted onto the train just before the doors closed.

There was a crash into the doors behind us. I turned.

It was Swordsman.

I smiled and gave him a little finger wave as the train started up and pulled away from the station.

Pearson looked at me and said, "Well! *That* was exciting! Wasn't it?"

I looked at him, smirked, and said, "It's good to see that someone still has the get up and go that started the Empire."

Pearson shrugged. "The get up and go all got up and went to the Catholic church. Trust me on that. I was part of the move."

Then Shifa crashed through the train window before the train moved into the first hallway. He crashed to the floor. The other passengers gasped and screamed as they backed away. He rose and turned on Pearson and me. His face was smashed up and covered in cuts.

And we could visibly see the gashes sealing up and the bones in his face resetting. He grinned.

Before he was done healing, I crashed into him, smashing him up against the wall of the train. I head-butted him, grabbed him by the lapels, then hauled him up and around as I threw him back out of the window. I wasn't worried about killing him. Shifa had decided that the best way to use his piece of the Soul Stone was to cause continuous, endless healing. Obviously, he had seen at least one X-Men movie with Hugh Jackman.

"So there," I spat in his direction. I looked back into the train. The other passengers were looking at me like I had grown horns. I jerked my thumb out to the broken window and said, simply, "No ticket."

Yes, I had wanted to use that line since I saw *Indiana Jones and the Last Crusade*. Especially since "crusader" was probably the next line on my CV.

Everyone went back to ignoring me.

There was just enough room on the train for Pearson and me to have a relatively sequestered conversation. It helped that when I sat down, everyone around us cleared out.

Instead of just running from one enemy to the other, we needed to know where the heck we were going. Not to mention that we hadn't even finished our last conversation.

"So, now what would be the next step?" I asked Pearson. "They have the Soul Stone. Fine. Assuming that it works as a WMD, what's the next step? What would you need to set it off?

Pearson smiled gently at me. We had already discussed the answer earlier. "Aside from will?"

I shook my head. He misunderstood me. "Too vague. That's *the trigger*. They'd need at least a test run before they could decide that it would work on cue ..." I stopped, thinking back to the crime scene. "Oh, wait, that supposed artillery damage at the museum. There were no fragments, just explosions, and melted asphalt. They can at least control the main stone, not just pieces."

Pearson raised a finger. "Yes, but wait a moment. The stone is supposed to wreck cities. The increase in violence has probably been a part of a plan to charge the stone further." He shrugged. "If you knew the stone thrived on misery and suffering, and you wanted it for nefarious purposes, wouldn't you do everything in your power to rev up the suffering of the average populace?"

I frowned. He had a point. "What now? Back to the Imam? See if Kozbar will cooperate with us?"

Pearson shrugged. "That's not a terrible idea. But we're already on the train to the Museum. Let's go through, see if we can get any more background on the Soul Stone. I think even a *rumor* would be helpful by now."

I nodded slowly. I didn't want to tell him that even I didn't think that going back to Whitechapel was a good idea. Mainly because I had the feeling that we'd get murdered if we went back there. No, not necessarily by whoever masterminded the theft of the Soul Stone. There could be some locals who already had our photograph and simply wanted to string us up because we offended them by asking some questions. Hell, just because Kozbar didn't flash our pictures around during his press conference with the mayor didn't mean that he didn't put out a Be On the Look Out photo for both of us.

Unfortunately, that meant that we were in trouble. Whoever was behind this wanted us dead. They also could turn foot soldiers into super villains.

Assuming that wasn't Kozbar, that meant we had a *second* force of the local Muslim population unhappy with us... if Kozbar *was* part of the main problem, then that meant he could create supervillains out of *anyone* in his congregation that he felt he could trust to kill two meddlers who threatened "the community (IE: Kozbar)." On that sliding scale, Kozbar could conceivably recruit parishioners who weren't even involved with the Soul Stone plot.

The police weren't on our side. Which, given the relative lack of rights in the United Kingdom (Right to Free Speech? Right to Bear Arms? What are those?) meant that Aaron Shaw of the Met could decide that we were a threat to public order and disappear us until after the city burns.

Worst of all were the shadows. The shadows that held me down while Swordsman tried to bisect me. The shadows that gathered in my hotel room to haunt me. The shadows of London were growing stronger, and I wondered how long it would take for them to get the timing right—trip me at the right moment, slow down a punch at the right time, shove me in front of traffic when it really mattered.

Shadows, cops, the population of Whitechapel, all piled on top of what we were trying to track down. This shouldn't completely and totally suck. I ...

I stopped thinking for a moment. The wind continued to blow in from the tunnel outside the train. The tunnel was dark and unlit...

Most of all, it was filled with shadows. *Aw nuts.*

"Pearson," I said softly. "I think we should get off at the next stop."

The darkness moved. The edges of the hole in the window faded, swallowed by the shadows. It bubbled and burbled, spilling over the edges, leaking into the train. The lights began to flicker.

Meaning the shadows were *eating* the illumination from the ceiling lights in the train.

Pearson looked at me, looked at the darkness outside, and patted me on the arm. "Wait here."

Pearson stood, pulling out a breviary. He stepped over to the shattered window and opened the book. He started to read aloud from his book of daily prayers.

The shadow's progress halted. It leaked down but stopped at only an inch away from the hole. More tried to flood in, looking like a giant bubble in an oil slick. But it fought against ... something. Pearson? Either way, it fell back, into the outer darkness.

Pearson stood, reading his breviary until the train pulled into the terminal. The main lights at the underground stop dispelled the darkness.

The doors opened. I grabbed Pearson and pulled him out of there and straight for the stairs. As soon as I stepped out to street level, the wind nearly knocked me sideways. After the shadows below, I had looked forward to a bright sunny day at noon. Instead, the sky was black. The clouds were so thick in the sky, they had completely and totally blotted out the sun and any ambient light. The heavy wind kept every flag flying straight. The temperature had dropped from "warm spring in Queens" to "winter" in the course of a train ride.

I pulled Pearson into the door frame of a building. "Tell me this is normal for London this time of year," I bellowed over the wind.

"Sorry!" he yelled back. "Can't."

The flags drooped a little, and we stepped out. The wind had died down enough for us to get moving. Though I was worried about where it would take us next. We had left a weather manipulator back at the Cathedral. Was this him and his power building up over the city? Were there several of them manipulating the weather? Or was it the Soul Stone? Had the rock fully charged, and this was the prelude to turning London into a crater?

Worst of all, the streets were full of shadows.

We ran throughout the city, dodging cars. We followed the instructions on the street—look left, look right, look diagonal, look up, look down, don't look, there's a bus coming, and you can't avoid it—and still nearly got hit a few times. After a few minutes of fighting the car and pedestrian traffic, I tried levitating... and it didn't work. I frowned. When we got to the corner, and a strong cross breeze, I experimented with a little hop. The wind increased. I think it even shifted me.

The wind is so strong, levitation may carry me away. Yay.

We pushed forward. The shadows warped and shifted, but they hadn't become corporeal yet. They were straining in their natural confines, slithering and writhing in place. Along sidewalks, and up the sides of buildings. The street lamps were of minimal use, as though the light bulbs were trying to fight the darkness. I drifted too close to the side of a building and felt the whisper of fingers clawing along my cheek. I jerked away and ran faster.

What are they waiting for? I wondered.

We came to a crosswalk and found a couple huddled over a cardboard sign asking for money. I took Pearson by the shoulders, pressed him into a doorway so he wouldn't get blown away. I loomed over the two of them and called out, "Get out of the street. It's only going to get worse."

The two homeless—who were teenagers, really—looked up at me like they were confused. "Was there a weather report?"

"I saw the storm front moving in," I answered honestly. I reached down to offer both of them a hand. I helped them both up and led them both to a nearby cafe. I pulled out a handful of coins, stared at it in confusion, and just handed it to both of them. Their eyes lit up.

We charged towards the Museum and struggled up the stairs. The craters in the street and grass were now pools of water, and the sidewalk was thick with water. The area must have had a serious rain storm while we were underground.

I pushed into the Museum.

Standing around the lobby like a committee meeting on its feet were Inspector Aaron Shaw and forty of his fellow cops from the Met.

Shaw turned to us and grinned. He held up his hand in a fist, making them all stand still. "Thank you for coming," he rumbled in his harsh, raspy voice. "It saves us time hunting you down later. Thomas Nolan, you are under arrest."

12

FURY OF THE STORM

I didn't say anything for a moment. I looked from one side to the other. He had a *lot* of cops. I didn't know what they were doing here in the first place.

"On what charge?" I asked calmly.

Shaw smiled. "Lord and Lady Fowler swore out a complaint against you. They've stated that you two stole explosives from the Fowler munitions company."

I blinked and looked at Pearson. "Can you imagine what we would do with explosives? I don't think I want to blow up anything in London yet."

Pearson leaned over and said, "The A0406. It's terrible. Unless you prefer highways. Then it's the M25."

I nodded sagely, rolling with the joke.

Shaw wasn't laughing. "We figure that you two are here to start a false flag terrorist attack to start a war. *Again*. Because that's what you Americans *do*, don't you? Investigating a lead about a threat to New York is just a cover, isn't it? What are you really? CIA?"

All humor drained out of the situation. Given his supposition and reinforcements, this wasn't the way he would go after a terrorist suspect.

Funny, if he was going to arrest us, you'd think he'd have had his men encircle us first so we couldn't run.

Then I realized that he wanted us to run. Half of his men were carrying guns, specially rolled out and issued just for us.

We were apparently so inconvenient to the city of London, someone wanted us dead...or maybe just me. It took me a moment to process this. Shaw must have read my face because he smiled. While I couldn't read his mind, I had the strong impression that if we went quietly, there would be an accident for at least one of us in holding.

If he wants us to run, let's give it to him. God, any ideas what I should be doing now? I'm figuring levitation would get us out the door, at least. Bi-location for a distraction?

Time slowed for me. Reality warped a little as my vision began to split. I was going to bi-locate.

Time to put on a show. "Are you sure that I'm here? Are you sure that I'm not over there?"

That's when two duplicates appeared behind the gathering of police officers.

Both of my duplicates grabbed the sidearms out of the holsters. I crashed both of them into the crowd, holding the stolen guns up into the air and firing repeatedly into the domed glass ceiling overhead. They emptied their magazines into the air. Then the duplicates faded out of existence, making everyone in the crowd of cops to whirl around for two people who technically never existed.

Shaw turned his head towards the gunshots and reached for his gun. Too late, he realized he was in trouble. He turned back to me, but too late. My left hand clamped down on his gun arm. My right drove a cross into his face. Shaw's head snapped back. As he fell, I came back with his 9mm Glock 26. I took the ten rounds and ran with it.

Mostly, I just ran.

Pearson and I ran for the front door.

We took two steps outside, and the rain started. It came down in sheets—and I mean sheet metal, not loose leaf. The first blast of rain felt like a cold, wet slap in the face. The individual raindrops felt like being pelted with pebbles. They even stung where they hit. You can imagine that a face full of rain felt more like landing face first in a cactus patch.

Pearson grabbed my arm. "Just follow me. I used to be a London cabby before ... before."

I didn't say anything, just followed the shiny bald head. My overcoat was soaked through before I reached the bottom of the steps. I was happy I could even see Pearson just a few feet in front of me. Even with my arm blocking the rain from my face, our push forward was as fast as a brisk walk. If this pace kept up, the cops would shoot us in the back before we could get to the curb.

I only had one prayer to hand that mentioned weather. Technically, it was more about artillery.

St Barbara, you are stronger than the tower of a fortress and the fury of hurricanes. Do not let lightning hit me, thunder frighten me or the roar of canons jolt my courage or bravery. Stay always by my side so that I may confront all the storms and battles of my life with my head held high and a serene countenance. Winning all the struggles, may I, aware of doing my duty, be grateful to you, my protector, and render thanks to God, the Creator of heaven, earth and nature who has the power to dominate the fury of the storm and to mitigate the cruelty of war.

The rain suddenly lessened. All around us, the downpour continued. As we ran, Pearson and I got droplets splashed in our direction by the wind, but that felt like a normal rain in comparison. We shot down the side street, then broke off into another side street that deviated by a sharp angle. The streets zigged, and we zagged.

Pearson charged along a street that was designed more like an alley. He crashed into a gathering of men at the end of the block. I got there in time for him to pick himself off the ground.

Then I noticed that these men were not being rained on, not even a little.

One pointed at me, eyes wide, and spewed out a string of Arabic. I heard two words clearly: "Nolan" and "Kozbar." I didn't think I needed a translation. I spun, smashing a hammer fist into the nearest young man. His homemade knife skittered out of his hand and into the street. I twisted back, plowing an uppercut into the stomach of the next nearest man, forcing him to double over.

The other three pulled out weapons. We had no time for such things. I grabbed the man I just decked and shoved him into the other three. I took Pearson by the arm and started running.

I got half a block before I tripped. I had the fainted glimpse when I fell of a thin line of shadow catching my toe in mid-stride. I hit the ground and rolled to my feet.

"Father! Watch out! The shadows are moving!"

Pearson skidded to a stop as a shadow leaped out from an alley. It tore the front of his shirt and slammed into a parked car, crumbling the side and knocking it out into a street, as though it had been T-boned by a truck. It whirled on Pearson and reared back. It had taken a shape of a large cat—a tiger. It made no sound as it came down and stalked towards Pearson.

I didn't stop running as I delivered a windmill punch screaming, "*Ad maiorem Dei gloriam.*"

I punched the shadow in the head. It recoiled. I pushed on, and Pearson charged after me. The armed thugs were closing. I decided they could deal with the shadow.

Then, shooting out into the street at a right-angle, was a police car, lights flashing.

The doors opened, and I poured on more speed. The driver only had one leg out of the car when he saw me coming. I slammed the door on his thigh. He screamed. I pulled out the Glock 26 from my pocket and jammed it in the driver's face. I looked to his passenger and said, "I really like your gun control laws here, where *you're* not even allowed to carry a gun. Get out."

The passenger got out of the car. I swung the door open, grabbed the driver, and tossed him out. "Father, you drive."

The driver scrambled backwards. Pearson kept an eye on him, I kept my eye on the passenger as I waved him over to join his friend.

The passenger's eyes widened in terror, and I whirled around, dropping to a knee.

The shadow had caught up to us, leading a pack of young Muslim men—ten of them. *They apparently got some friends*, I thought.

I didn't think it would do any good but zipped through a prayer in my head and leveled the gun at the shadow beast.

Lord, you gave Saint Gabriel of Our Lady of Sorrows a special privilege of entering into the passion of Your Son and into the compassion of his Virgin Mother, Mary. Teach us to contemplate with his eyes the very mystery of salvation and to grow in love in the spirit of joy. Amen.

I fired. The shadow flinched at the strike. The bullet went through it and into one of the hoodlums leading the pack chasing us.

I leaped into the car, and Pearson peeled off.

"Nice shot," Pearson complimented me.

I shrugged as I kept an eye on the world around us. The rain still kept coming down, though not as heavily on the car or the windshield.

"I don't think it was me. I said a quick one to Saint Gabriel of Our Lady of Sorrows."

Pearson took a moment and laughed. The story goes that Francesco Possenti was a monk who once faced down a collection of over twenty of Garibaldi's Red Shirts in 1860. The soldiers invaded Isola, Italy, and promptly started to rob, rape, and pillage. Possenti walked into the center of town to face the terrorists. Possenti yanked the gun out of the belt of a would-be rapist and told the Red Shirt to release the girl. As another Red Shirt came by, Possenti grabbed *his* revolver, too.

During the commotion, the other Red Shirts charged the position.

At that moment, a lizard ran between Possenti and the Red Shirts. Possenti struck the lizard with one shot. Dual-wielding, Possenti commanded the Red Shirts to drop their weapons. The soldiers complied rather than test his aim. Possenti marched them out of town.

"The story about Possenti might be apocryphal, but I didn't have anything else to go with."

Six police cars shot out into the street in front of us. I immediately looked out my window, to the left.

The street lamps were out, and what little I could see of the homes down the street were being consumed by a wave of utter darkness.

13

EYE OF THE STORM

"Turn *right*," I called.

Pearson did so without a problem.

Down that street was an angry mob. *I'll take it*, I thought. I reached over and grabbed the wheel, then reached over and stomped down on the accelerator. The mob disbursed, scrambling out of our way. I knew that, when faced with a police car that *wouldn't* stop for them, they would not call my bluff.

Then again, I wasn't bluffing—I had my eyes closed.

"Give me that!" Pearson snapped.

I let go and looked behind us. The wave of darkness raced forward, running over the mob. I didn't see if they were consumed, or just hidden by the lack of light, but either way, I wasn't going to worry about it.

Pearson took the wheel back, made a sharp turn up Drury Lane (coming off of Parker Street, which went one way the wrong way—oops) and a left on Short's Garden.

We circled around through multiple back streets, and parked the car near Saint Anne's Church ("Church of England," Pearson said. "Serves them right if they get raided.") and walked three blocks to Saint Patrick's Church in Soho Square. It was a nice, simple, red brick building, one of the first Catholic churches built after Henry VIII made his own church for his own ends.

After we dried out and the pastor gave us a quick bite to eat, we met in the rectory. Outside, the rain continued, unabated. I honestly expected windows to crack with every gust of wind.

Pearson clapped his hands together and smiled. "That was brisk. Wasn't it?"

I sat at the table in the corner. "How about we start with you?"

The smile dimmed only a little. The eyes went from wide, bright and shiny to narrow and cynical. They were cat's eyes. "Oh really?"

I smiled at him. "Yes. Really. What are you? And if you say combat exorcist and former cabby, I'm going to start making my way home, even if I have to swim."

Pearson sat, leaned back in his chair, and said, "MI-6. Happy now?"

I nodded slowly. It at least explained how he got us into MI-5 without a problem. Also how he knew how to play the Metropolitan police bureaucracy.

"When did you drive a cab?"

"A few years while I was at the seminary."

I nodded slowly. "Then, as an MI-6 officer, give me your assessment of what we just went through out there."

"I won't even speculate on the shadows," Pearson said. "We can only presume they're connected to the Soul Stone. The police ... I don't think I need to mention that Fowler and Toynbee are behind this somehow?"

I shook my head. There was no reason for them to make a fake police report against us for stealing explosives *unless* they were up to no good. It was theoretically possible that the Lord and Lady were up to some *unrelated* nefarious scheme that they thought I might trip over during my investigation, but that was unlikely.

"And Kozbar?"

Pearson frowned. "That's more of a tough one. He could be tied in with all this, it might just be good timing on his part. Who knows? The Soul Stone might be able to influence susceptible people into unleashing their natural anger, and Kozbar had just hidden it well up to this point." Pearson slid off his glasses and pinched his nose. "You know one of the reasons I haven't been part of the 'ship back all of them' crowd? There are too many miracles among the refugees from the Middle East. There are scores of Marian visions among them. Too many refugees have been unleashed from their prison and allowed out into the light. We've had a rash of baptisms. There have been hundreds of thousands of them across Europe, and the UK.

"But on the other hand, those are hidden among millions of people. Unfortunately, this is only 10% of them. I would dearly love for the race riots, the sharia, the terrorism to stop. But I do fear tossing the baby out with the bathwater. But you know how Europe works. It's either trying for a socialist utopia, or strapping up their jackboots. They have no concept of what a 'middle' looks like. They have less idea of what Libertarians are."

I smiled. "The Warlock who tried to destroy me and everyone around me was a Libertarian. They're not necessarily all that they're cracked up to be. At least not by that name. I suspect a European Libertarian would be the wrong kind."

"What kind is that?"

"The kind that says 'Believe and act as you will, as long as you agree with me.'"

"And you?"

"I'm of the 'leave me alone, I'll leave you alone unless you need help' school."

Pearson nodded and studied me a moment. Once he seemed satisfied, he said, "If we're done with me?"

I nodded, my curiosity sated. "Fowler and Toynbee."

Pearson sighed, relieved. "Yes. "Well, obviously the Fowlers are bad guys."

I nodded. "Yes, they were the only people that knew I was at the Cathedral for the rioters to show up this morning. That's on top of the false police report."

"Any idea of what their goal is?" Pearson asked.

I thought back to my conversation with them. Atheists or not, I couldn't imagine a good reason for them to be involved in a plot with a mystical artifact utilizing magic that could annihilate the city *they* lived in. "No idea. But we'll just have to stop them. Who cares *what* their problem is."

Pearson laughed. He shook his head, entertained. "Okay, fine then, mister American, answer this one at least—Where would the best place for the soul stone be? If they were going to absorb all of the misery and assaults in the city?"

I shrugged. It was obvious to me, at least. "I don't know why you're asking me. You're the expert. But I'd figure the easy place would be the center of town."

Pearson blinked, tilted his head, and frowned. "According to Legend, the Soul Stone just needs to be *within* the city. Not anywhere specific."

I scoffed. "Yeah? And? You told me Saddam had it in the torture chambers of a palace. Human beings like physical proximity, just in case. Humor me. What's the center of London?"

"Technically, it's in a church. However, that church overlooks Trafalgar Square."

I stood. "Let's go out and get it then."

Pearson held up a hand. He reached into his pocket and pulled out a cell phone. He played with it for a few minutes. "The weather's bad." He played with it for a few more minutes. "Traffic is a pain in the arse. Flash flood warnings. Warnings to stay out of the underground."

The phone then blared with an alarm that sounded like something from the emergency alert system, in case of nuclear bombs. Pearson tapped his phone a few more moments, and his eyes widened.

"So, do you think anyone will know you're the source of a race riot?"

14

THROUGH THE FIRE AND FLAMES

"What riot?" I asked.

Pearson turned the phone around and showed me the screen. The main page of BBC News was a video of riots and blood in the street. Molotov cocktails, rocks, and bricks flew into windows, statues, buildings, and beatings in the street.

Underneath the video stream read a crawl, reading "IMAM KOZBAR CALLS FOR SLEEPLESS NIGHT FOR LONDON," followed by "RACE RIOT THROUGHOUT LONDON," and ended in "KOZBAR CITES RACISM, ABUSE, AS CAUSE OF UNREST."

I rolled my eyes. *Ask a guy some questions, defend yourself against some of his parishioners, you're an abusive racist. Yay. If I wanted this sort of BS, I'd've stayed in New York.*

I handed the phone back to Pearson. "Great. Just great. You'd think that the weather would suppress rioting at least a little."

Pearson turned the phone screen back to me. He said nothing for a moment. It took me that long to notice that the rain on the rioters was not the rain on the roof. Whoever had been controlling the weather had enough practice to wield it on individual groups.

Okay, this might be problematic. "What about the path between here and Trafalgar Square?"

Pearson frowned. I could almost hear him working out the path, discounting the underground because of flooding, and discounting cars because he wouldn't want to run over the rioters in our way.

"It's only a little over a half a mile," Pearson finally said. "Normally, it's a twelve- or fifteen-minute walk."

"But there's rioting."

Pearson nodded. "But there's rioting."

"Has anyone mapped the rioting?"

Pearson flipped through his phone for another minute. He nodded. "The closer you get to Trafalgar, the worse it's going to get. I'm not all that surprised. I have no idea how much of this has been planned, or how much the Soul Stone itself is prompting people into mass destruction."

I nodded and stood. "Time to get wet again."

Pearson frowned. "Pardon me, but we should probably get a poncho first. I'm certain they should have a few somewhere."

I rolled my eyes.

Within fifteen minutes, we were back out on the street in bright yellow ponchos.

Surprisingly, it didn't take us long to get through the rioting. The rioters weren't interested in people so much as they were in property damage and shopping with a brick. Neither Pearson nor I were interested in trying to hold back the tide against property. While I felt for those people who had their possessions damaged or their businesses burned, there was also the slightest bit of schadenfreude on my part. Honestly, it was less that I enjoyed the suffering of others, and more that I enjoyed the irony of a people who had sacrificed their rights to bear weapons of any type, be it a handgun or a kitchen knife, to having their lives turned upside down by people who didn't care about their laws.

And yes, I do recognize the problem in that statement. I live in New York, which is trying to do the same thing. The moment anyone told me to do house-to-house gun confiscation would be the day I set up an underground armed resistance.

On the way to Trafalgar Square, though, Pearson and I had a few incidents.

When a small wave of shadows came for us, I snatched the Molotov cocktail from the hand of a rioter and threw it in front of them. The shadows reared back and made a sound like a cross between nails on a blackboard and hoard of dying farm animals being brutally slaughtered.

I spun back towards the rioter and punched him in the face before he could shank me.

I whirled back to the path. I started praying and ran.

The light of God surrounds us, The love of God enfolds us—

We ran. We saw a group of girls beset by rioters. The men grabbed at their clothes, then at their arms. Two girls had been peeled off already and thrown to the ground. Each girl had at least four men stripping her.

The power of God protects us, The presence of God watches over us—

I didn't even need to ask God for help. I bi-located immediately. It was less of a bi- and more of a sex-located. All five of my duplicates piled into the rioters while the one running alongside Pearson kept going. I stole knives from them and slashed their thigh muscles, rammed knife points into kneecaps, and slit throats. One of me even stole a bottle of acid from a rioter and poured it in his eyes, then flung the bottle like I was dispensing holy water in the asperges ritual on the congregation during mass. It resulted in little more than a sprinkling, but it got their attention. Then all of me drew the gun stolen from earlier and opened fire. The rioters fled one way, the girls another.

It was over in seconds.

Wherever we are, God is, And where God is, all is well.

But then I heard cries for help coming from different directions. All around, the rioters had encountered other citizens and started the next phase of the attack—people.

St. Matthew, St. Mark, St. Luke, St. John, Like unto the prophet Jonas, as a type of Christ—

Then, I—we—split up.

I went East, gun drawn. A gathering of homeless were being beaten by the rioters. I opened fire, driving them off. I gave their victims directions to Saint Patrick's Catholic church. They took the information and ran. The rioters came back with friends. I fended them off until my gun ran dry. They didn't even let me get close enough to go melee before throwing six Molotov cocktails at me at once. I went up in a blaze, consumed in fire as I burned alive. I even felt the burning gasoline down my throat as it consumed me inside and out.

Who was guarded for three days and three nights in the belly of a whale—

I went West, gun drawn. Three rioters held a father of two down on the sidewalk as his children watched them tease him with dripping acid on the ground around him. I dropped to one knee, took careful aim, and fired at the one with the acid. I blew his brains out, causing him to tilt into one of his friends, spilling acid over his buddy. I targeted the unwounded one and shot him. The father struggled to his feet when shadows reached up from the street and grabbed him. It took him by the ankles and dragged him across the sidewalk, pulling him into an alley. I ran faster, jumped over the father, and stomped on the tendrils of shadow. It speared me through the sides, the palms of both hands, and through both feet before wrapping around my torso, wrists, and ankles before it dragged me into the darkness. There was much wailing (mine) and gnawing of teeth (not mine) as the shadow tore into my bi-located form. I felt every moment of it. I waited until the family had gotten away before that form faded away.

Thus shall the Almighty God, As a Father, guard and protect me from all evil.

I went north, back the way we came. The riot had expanded in behind us. One gang had broken through a door and threw the owners into the street so they could be beaten. I opened fire with my stolen handgun, emptying it into the crowd. The shock and the dead bodies pushed back the crowd from a family. They got up and ran past me. I held the gun up as though I still had bullets in it and held the riot back. This lasted a whole thirty seconds before they started throwing bricks at me. I figured as long as they kept up the brick throwing, they weren't chasing after other people... then a brick clipped me in the head. I went down and faded away.

Grant, O Lord, Thy protection And in protection, strength—

Another one of me also went north. I collected a series of homeless out on the street and herded them back towards the church, which was hopefully still out of the riot zone. I even collected the families I saved during the other encounters. I led point, shooting at any rioters in our way. When someone's head exploded from the impact of a bullet, the other rioters scattered like bullets were contagious. I led them to the edge of the riot zone when one of the shadows tripped me and dragged me off. The last coherent words past those lips were "RUN!" I didn't fade away this time. I stayed until my head was crushed by jagged shadowy teeth.

I also brought up the rear of the refugees from the rioters. The rioters were following. After the me leading the front of the crowd had been snagged by darkness, I stopped and turned to face the rioters. I dropped to one knee and shot one of the mob leaders. He went down, trampled, and I held my fire for five seconds, long enough for people in the mob to realize they were tripping over one of their own—and that he'd been shot. They broke up, spreading out in an arc around me. You can imagine how long it takes for a mob to do that. One of them tried to pass me on the right, edging along the buildings. I swung towards him and shot him. I swung back to the main body and said, "Who's next?" It took them five minutes to test me, wear out my ammunition, then close on me. At the end of the night, that form of mine was beaten to death with cricket bats.

And in strength, understanding. And in understanding, knowledg—

By the time Pearson and I made it to Trafalgar Square, all of my bi-located forms were killed off and faded away.

Unfortunately, the rest of the riot had centered at the square. Cars were overturned and on fire, forming a barricade. One of the double-decker buses was also aflame.

And in knowledge, the knowledge of justice. And in the knowledge of justice, the love of it—

Most importantly, someone was climbing down from the Admiral Nelson statue at the top of Trafalgar Square. And he had the Soul Stone.

And in the love of it, the love of all existences. And in that love, the love of spirit and all creation. Amen.

15

RAIDERS

The wind picked up again once the man with the Soul Stone had hit the ground. The rioters broke up, moving out of the way of the Soul Stone and its carrier.

I wondered exactly just how much the stone was influencing the mob.

We ran for the Soul Stone, but the lightning flashed again, snapping just in front of us. We came up short before another lightning strike hit the exact same place.

That doesn't happen naturally, I thought. I reached out and grabbed Pearson by the collar and pulled him back. I looked up, scanning the rooftops for the weather-controlling Jihadi.

I spotted him on top of the national gallery. He looked like a bearded marshmallow man. His evil laughter cackled over the night sky. I took aim at him, and he pointed at me. I dove to one side in time to avoid the lightning strike. I heard the thunder boom. I even heard the sizzle.

I rolled again on instinct. The lightning struck where I had been. I kept it up, running, zigging, zagging, diving, rolling, bouncing around Trafalgar Square like a ping-pong ball.

You may well wonder why I wasn't running for the National Gallery. If I pressed up against the building, I couldn't be targeted.

But then I couldn't distract him from the copy that bi-located behind him and shot him in the back of the head.

The Jihadi fell from the National Gallery and landed with a *splat*.

I let my copy fade away back into one of me. Pearson ran up to my side now that I wasn't being chased by lightning. I holstered my gun and looked around the square. The riot really had broken up—or had at least moved on. The square had been packed with a noisy, angry riot setting things on fire, turning over cars, and calling for blood. They even had a supernatural light show where it looked like Allah himself was trying to light up an infidel—and if they had looked closely, the infidel that Kozbar had taken such offense to. They should have stayed and watched me get deep fried. Instead, they fled.

The entire square was empty. The Soul Stone was gone. The Jihadists were gone. The rioters were gone. Everyone was gone.

But I knew one thing. There was no way that the Jihadists knew that tonight would be the time to get to the Soul Stone. The riot had covered their retrieval. But how could they have been prepared to get to the stone through a riot? How could they have known that this riot would happen this way, on this day, and that there would be a massive crowd to disappear into?

The only way they would have known is if they knew that someone would whip the crowd up into a frenzy and spark a riot. And only one man could have predicted that there would have been a riot – the one who sparked it.

Kozbar.

I narrowed my eyes, anger rising within me. I had given that bastard the presumption of innocence. What I should have done was consider everyone guilty until proved otherwise. Then again, I assumed everyone was good inside until they tried to shiv me, so either way, I would have lost that bet.

"Kozbar's in on it."

Pearson nodded, without even asking me about my conclusion.

"The timing of the riot and the retrieval of the stone do seem to be suspicious."

I looked at Pearson like he was insane for such an understatement. He merely smiled at me and shrugged, causing droplets to fall off of his windbreaker. Pearson said, "So, what now?"

I frowned. I considered the sudden quiet. After thunder in my ears and running through a riot, the calm felt unnatural. Despite the death of the weather Jihadi, there was still a sun-blackening sky overhead. I glanced at my watch. It was still only three in the afternoon, and it looked closer to three in the morning.

I closed my eyes and thought a moment. Then I found I couldn't think. My mind raced with everything that had bounced around my brain for the past few hours. There was Fowler and Toynbee from this morning, the riot, the police officers hunting me, the shadows hunting us, the rioters, the Soul Stone, and realizing that Fowler, Toynbee, and Kozbar were all together in one massive, insane plot that made no sense.

I took a breath and said a quick prayer to one of the two Tommies I'd been baptized under – Thomas Aquinas.

Come, Holy Spirit, Divine Creator, the true source of light and fountain of wisdom. Pour forth your brilliance upon my intellect, dissipate the darkness which covers me, that of sin and of ignorance. Grant me a penetrating mind to understand, a retentive memory, method and ease in learning, the lucidity to comprehend, and abundant grace in expressing myself. Guide the beginning of my work, direct its progress, and bring it to successful completion. This I ask through Jesus Christ, true God and true man, living and reigning with You and the Father, forever and ever. Amen.

My mind cleared.

The short version was that there was no way to guess where the stone would end up after I saw it in the square. Between Toynbee, Fowler, and Kozbar, the Soul Stone could be hidden any number of places. It could be in the Whitechapel complex, in one of a hundred rooms in the Muslim center complex. It could be hidden in The Museum. It could be in a business run by the Fowlers, or Kozbar could have passed it off to another Imam at another mosque, who had no connection to the master plan they had cooking up.

Which meant there was only one option left.

Dear God, if there is another way, please let me find it. But otherwise, please, I need to be able to find the Soul Stone. I presume it must reek of evil to such an extent that even in this city of darkness, its scent must be the most foul. So, if there is no other way, please give me back my charism to smell evil in all its—

The prayer was answered before I even finished. The scent of sin and evil filled my nostrils without any warning. I snapped my head away from Pearson and vomited into the nearest puddle. I breathed in again and vomited again. Then the dry heaves kicked in, making it feel like my guts were going to come out next.

I breathed through my mouth, though that wasn't much better.

I straightened and tried to take shallow breaths. I looked at Pearson and said, "Come on, let's go."

I started walking. The scent took me south. We walked for the first ten minutes, but after watching me scarper around for a while, Pearson went on ahead and rented two bicycles for us.

We biked for the next hour, going from the city of London to "Outer London." We ended up in the London Borough of Croydon, in South London. It was fairly large, at over thirty-three square miles, and is the London borough with the most population. In the middle was the historic town of Croydon. Formerly a small market town, it expanded into the most populous areas.

Croydon looked ... nice. It was one part early modern and one part ultra-modern, with a scattering of every era in-between. Some of the older brick buildings looked like they would have looked at home in the middle of a little German village (probably for tourists). A lot of them were Victorian, some were so early 20th century, they could have been some places in New York.

The smell led me to a tower. It was massive. It was Empire State Building tall, about ninety stories tall. It was glass and steel. It was even less festive than my home town's "Freedom Tower," which at least had a few angles to it. This was more like a glass box with an attitude problem.

We circled the block once so I could confirm where the Soul Stone was hidden.

"Certain?" Pearson asked.

I nodded. The smell was strongest at the tower. Pearson nodded. Before I did something idiotic and charged directly in, we withdrew to the nearest cafe.

The first thing we did was to do an Internet search on the owner of the tower.

Pearson flinched at his first result. "It was built over the ruins of Carfax Abby? I thought that was made up for *Dracula*."

I rolled my eyes and sighed. "Eh. My life feels like a Universal monster film, so why not?"

Pearson shrugged. "Would you like to guess who owns it?"

"Dame Polly Toynbee, and Lord Newby Fowler."

"However did you know?"

16

FAITH OF THE FATHERLESS

S ince I couldn't wrap my brain around what reason on God's green Earth could have prompted Toynbee and Fowler to have Jihadists steal an artifact that could destroy the city, I did a quick Internet search via Duck Duck Go.

The first five entries covered their businesses—politics, museum curators, manufacturing, and journalism—and the next ten were about all of their charities. They were "pro-LGGBDTTTIQQAAPP"... which was the extended version of L.G.B.T.M.O.U.S.E. (if you care, it stands for "Lesbian, Gay, Genderqueer, Bisexual, Demisexual, Transgender, Transsexual, Twospirit, Intersex, Queer, Questioning, Asexual, Allies, Pansexual, Polyamorous" and a partridge in a pear tree). They were "pro-refugee" and "pro-immigration," and had been a large supporter of bringing in more refugees into every nation, especially London and Germany.

A few more minutes of searching Duck Duck Go (which I presume is "ducking" for short ... which meant that searching for yourself was "go duck yourself"), I got a bit more of the stories. Because *not only* were Fowler and Toynbee pro-sex, they were pro-sex for everybody, at any age—the headline read that they supported "the classical view of sex advocated by Plato," but the small print in the middle of a paragraph quickly mentioned that Plato's *Republic* discussed the proper way to court and seduce twelve-year-olds. Being pro-refugee and -immigration wasn't about *every* refugee and immigrant—only Muslims. If a refugee or immigrant was Buddhist, Kurd, Christian, white or Tibetan, then they were just flat out of luck. They had actively campaigned against allowing non-Muslims *out* of the Middle East, and those were the groups being annihilated.

Another charity was to "support immigrants suffering against racism"—which, in their particular case, meant slipping money to the Rotherham sex slave ring.

I slipped my phone away and leaned back in the chair of the cafe. "You know, it's called original sin. One of these days, I want these people to consider something original. These talking points could have been out of Mayor Hoynes' platform."

Pearson cocked his head, looking at me quizzically for a moment before he nodded. "Understood." He smoothed out his parka. "Shall we have at it? The tower. The infiltration?"

I nodded slowly. I didn't really know from breaking and entering. While I theoretically could pull it off with an apartment or a house, I wasn't an expert in raiding office buildings. Everything I knew about spying could be summed up by spy media. Even though I had a genuine former spy across the table from me, I didn't think it would be that good an idea to just walk in the front door.

It took me a moment, but I ran through the other ideas. If I levitated towards the floor with the Soul Stone, I could smell which floor it was on, then smash through a window with the pistol. If I bilocated directly to the floor with the stone, I could grab it, and maybe just fade away, bringing it away with me.

Either version would have me run smack into the other guards around the stone, and they would fill me so full of lead that I would sink immediately when they tossed my body into the river.

Then it hit me.

I stood. "Father, I'm going to need you to come with me. We have some prep work to do before we go in."

Two hours later, I walked into the front lobby of Toynbee Tower, flashed my badge at the front desk, and said, "Tell Fowler and Toynbee that Tommy Nolan, NYPD, wants to have a conversation with them."

FATHER PEARSON WAITED OUTSIDE as I waited for the front desk to pass my conversation up the chain of command. His purpose was to cover my ass in case Fowler and Toynbee were different than the other pricks I had gone up against. Because if they were smart, they would have gunmen pour out of every nook and cranny, mow me down with automatic fire from machine guns, then drop my body somewhere in the center of the rioting. My body would be written off as an unfortunate death of a nosy tourist with delusions of investigative adequacy.

Except there was one thing I had noticed in my dealings with pure evil. Despite having fought a demon, the President of a major political and business powerhouse, as well as a warlock with the ability to level buildings and sweep away armored forces, they all had one thing in common.

That one thing was the inability to shut the Hell up. The demon broke into my home, held my family at knifepoint, and would later start a riot—and the first thing it did was lecture at me. The leader of the death cult had me at her mercy and her first act? To gloat. Mayor Hoynes, warlock? Instead of crashing the house I was in down upon me, he unleashed his shadow matter, slapped me around ... and gloated.

I had caught a definitive pattern in MO. If I didn't know better, I would have declared right then and there that evil was, by its very nature, insecure and desperate to be understood.

If I believed in pop psychology, that would have been my diagnosis. It was more likely that evil was naturally self-obsessed and narcissistic, requiring them to brag at every available opportunity.

The elevator behind the front desk *pinged*. I leaned over, ready to reach for the handgun I carried.

Two uniformed rent-a-Bobbies came out. They were big and

brainless. One said, "Nolan?" in a cockney so thick, even Dick van Dyke in *Mary Poppins* would tell him to try again.

I nodded and went along with them.

They walked me into the elevator. It was strangely against a wall of the building instead of through the center, like most elevators. One guard took his security card, swiped it, and hit the button for floor forty-five.

As we traveled up, I mentally ran through the rosary, being certain to keep my breathing calm and steady. I didn't want to trigger the guards into acting prematurely, but I also didn't want to be taken off guard.

But when the elevator slowed to a stop, the doors opened, and they waved me out. I stepped out, the doors closed, and the elevator with the guards still on it.

The hallway was the size of a loft apartment. It was heavily deco-rated. It alternated between statues, art pieces, and fancy full-length mirrors. The floors and walls were marble. The floor was a smoothly-streaked ivory marble parquet, and the walls were cloudy pinkish variegated marble, almost overwhelming the white marble statues. The statues were nude classical Greeks at play, from young nymph girls to a convincing replica of The Athlete. Who knew, maybe The Museum housed the replica, and this was the real thing. In pride of place, a diminutive statue of Ganymede sat on a pedestal in the center, close to where it met the larger space. The attractive young boy held up a delicate cup in a startling mockery of the Eucharistic Blessing. I averted my eyes and focused on the more benign looking march of wall décor. The wall paintings were washes of color and mood in bright but modern gilt frames. They displayed vague arran-gements of vegetation and buildings from a past where golden suns-hine did a poor job of defining edges, but the colors were lurid splashy pastels. The collection matched the walls, at least. The endless hallway was amplified by the fact that every other wall frame was a large mirror hung in the same type frame that housed the paintings.

Check off the narcissist box.

I walked down the hallway calmly. I was almost surprised that the guards hadn't frisked me. But then again, everyone expected the anti-gun laws to work.

At the end of the hall was a massive chamber that took up the center of the building. *This explains the placement of the elevators.*

The chamber was also filled with armed Jihadi wannabes, complete with the black flag of ISIS and the typical ninja-style black hoods and pajamas often seen during beheading videos. The guns they carried were mostly AK-47s, with a smattering of other automatic rifles. Unfortunately, they all had their fingers on triggers, and they held their guns in a number of different ways—cross body (pointed at each other), held by the rifle butt (pointed at the ceiling) and at the ready (mostly at me, but it amounted to a circular firing squad).

One of them was behind Fowler and Toynbee, his gun pointed at the floor, his finger *off* the trigger. He was the only one.

At the opposite end of the chamber was a wide double desk, with Fowler and Toynbee behind it. They had large comfortable executive chairs that were more like thrones. Behind them were massive windows that covered from floor to ceiling. The chamber was so large, two of the four walls were windows.

The rest of the decorations were reminiscent of a country estate and a museum. If they were religious, I would have said that they had raided a temple and took souvenirs. Some of the plaques that I could read included "Taken from Santorini (Atlantis)" underneath a trident, or "found in Prague" under a stone arm. There was a statue of a monster that said "Property of the Museum of Natural History." A stone had a plaque that read "from the Walls of Sodom."

"For atheists, I'd normally think you'd be less superstitious," I said aloud. "But you guys seem more superstitious than pagans I know."

Fowler smiled broadly, his eyes hooded like he was half-asleep. He stood and spread his arms wide. "Inspector! How nice of you to come and join us."

I looked around at all of the ISIS knockoffs. "How could I miss the party?" I looked at the smart Jihadi behind their desk and behind them. "Especially since my favorite Imam was going to be here."

The Jihadi paused for a moment and gave a brief laugh. He reached up and pulled off his mask. Imam Kozbar smiled at me and gave a little bow. I looked around, and two other Jihadis pulled off their masks—Bariq and Shifa, the one who threw lightning bolts and the other one who just wouldn't die.

I looked at them. "While I waited to get here, I looked up your names. Lightning and healing? You guys really do think you're X-Men, don't you?"

Fowler gave a big theatrical sigh as he walked up to me. He stopped a reasonable conversation distance away. He must have assumed his friends would aim well if I made a move. "Oh, Inspector, you just don't get us at all, do you?"

I shook my head. "No. I don't. You know, for a bunch of atheists, you believe in a soul stone? You're working with Jihadists?"

Toynbee sighed from behind the desk. "How droll."

Fowler's eyes narrowed. They were less asleep and more the hooded vipers. "Yes. Quite the droll little Catholic copper, aren't you?" He shook his head, disappointed. "Oh, we don't *believe* in this sort of thing, you know."

I flinched, taken aback. I looked over the two of them, and they seemed sane ... and bored. "Then what exactly do you think you're doing?" I asked. "You take an artifact that claims mystical properties and the ability to destroy a city, charged solely by suffering, misery, and death, and you teamed up with armed Jihadists to steal it and use parts of it. If you told me you were art thieves and stole it yourself, it would make more sense."

Toynbee sat back in her chair. "Our alliance with Imam Kozbar is simple. He's helped us get artifacts out of the region before. And he has goals similar to ours."

I nodded slowly, humoring the deranged criminals with armed minions. "You got it out of Iraq in the first place. Why hand it over to the Museum if you were just going to steal it again?"

Fowler shrugged. "A miscalculation on our part. We didn't realize what the Soul Stone really was until after we turned it in as a valued cultural relic."

"And what is that? You said the Soul Stone isn't what I think it is?"

Fowler nodded, happy to pontificate. "It's in a Rose Cut pattern. That's the sort of thing requiring modern technology. There are no tool marks on it. That's impossible, even by today's standards. The legends say that Anubis came from the underworld to personally hand it to the first dynasty Pharaohs. What does that tell you?"

I looked at him stupidly for a moment, and I internally groaned at what his conclusion was going to be. "Any sufficiently advanced technology is indistinguishable from magic?"

Fowler laughed joyfully and spread his arms, happy that I had reached the "correct" conclusion. "Yes! Of course! It's *obvious*. This 'soul stone' is merely alien technology!"

I looked back and forth from Fowler to Kozbar. Kozbar seemed bored by Fowler's ranting. I asked, "And the idea that it runs on suffering?"

Fowler dismissed it with a wave of his hands. "Oh, that's easy to explain. The human brain undergoes certain brain wave changes when they feel pain or anguish, and dies. That's all. There's nothing magical or demonic about this toy. What sort of people do you think we are anyway?"

I involuntarily laughed and spread my hands at the Jihadists. "I think you're the sort of people who would level a city for fun."

Toynbee tittered. "Oh, not for *fun*, dear boy." She rose from behind the desk and walked over to join her husband and me. "Oh, of course, we're getting rid of London and the royal family. Being Anglican is all about political power. That's all it's ever been about. That's why the royals officially run the church. We *all* know there's no God, but it comes in handy. It's good for running the masses. The opiate of the people, don't you know?"

Fowler nodded as his wife joined him at his side, added, "But dear me, even some of the royals have married Catholics."

Toynbee shuddered in disgust. "As for the citizenry, well, they're going Catholic in droves. Droves! Whole parishes."

Fowler shook his head sadly. "We can't have that. We're going to alienate the tolerant, peaceful Muslims. Like Kozbar."

My mind went full *blue screen of death* for a moment. The stupidity so overwhelmed me, I couldn't process it for a moment.

By the time I tuned back in, Toynbee was saying, "... even worse, the Royal family might actually make us give *back* everything that our ancestors stole from the Catholic church over 500 years ago."

I paused, then nodded. Money motives were at least something I could wrap my brain around. But their ideas of what was a good plan was ... moronic. "So you'll nuke London for going Catholic, but align yourself with people who will cut off the head of those who disagree with them." I looked at Kozbar and snarked, "No offense."

Kozbar shrugged. "None taken."

I looked back to the two Brits. "You guys are just *so* chock full of tolerance."

Fowler and Toynbee exchanged a glance, then back to me. "Of course we're tolerant," Fowler said. "Just ask our charities."

I rolled my eyes. "I saw your press releases. Your 'pro-gay' support is all about sleeping with children."

Fowler shook his head. "No. You misunderstood. All men are secretly gay. Hetero is just something imposed upon them by cultural and societal pressures."

Toynbee nodded. "Dealing with children just makes it easier to break the conditioning of society."

Fowler shrugged. "Make them enjoy themselves often enough, they'll realize their true nature."

Toynbee looked at her husband. "Or they're so ashamed they enjoyed it, they run full into their true nature."

Fowler smiled dotingly at her. "True, that."

The words *Are you fucking kidding me?* didn't even begin to cover what was going through my head.

Fowler looked at me and waved at his Jihadi buddies. "And yes, of course! Our fellows agree with us when it comes to boys. Not girls just yet, but we'll get them there in the end. We're right, after all. Not that there's any such thing as objective right and wrong. But we're definitely correct."

I felt so ill, I wanted them to just shoot me and get it over with. "What are you going to do with me?"

From the window, Kozbar finally spoke. "Let's see if the soul stone will vaporize you."

Fowler glanced back at the Imam for a moment, paused, then laughed. "Yes! Splendid idea!" He looked back at me. "You see if it's powerful enough to destroy a city... well, you can see what happens with just a small fleck is embedded in the skin. Or in a weapon."

I nodded. "I noticed. You sure it's at full strength after breaking off pieces from it?"

"Oh, they grew back. It's one of the reasons why it was in Trafalgar Square. It takes a lot of energy for matter-energy conversion. And we spent a lot of time causing people to suffer."

17

GETTING STONED

Kozbar left the room to grab the Soul Stone. I looked around the room and calculated my odds. Even if everything went to my very sketchy plan, odds were that I wasn't going to make it out of the room.

I slipped my hands in my pockets and waited. Shooting all of them was unfeasible. Unless I bi-located four times, I wouldn't even have enough bullets.

Kozbar came back with the stone in his hands. I had to admit, it was pretty. The high-gloss obsidian sheen was mesmerizing, and the embedded glyphs looks like silver on one side and rubies on the other. As Kozbar held it, the red glyphs thrummed with a red glow.

Then Kozbar confused me. He offered me the stone.

Fowler's eyes widened and stepped forward, holding up a hand. "What are you doing?"

I concurred, confused. There had to be a trap in there somewhere. "Aren't you afraid that I'm going to use it on you?"

"Only those who are worthy may wield it," Kozbar said with all earnestness. He allowed himself a smile. "Not you, infidel. No infidels could use it."

I remembered the witnesses at The Museum saying that the first thief to grab the stone doubled over in pain. But whoever did it survived. That evening, I had been stabbed through the hands, feet, side, torso, impaled, burned alive and beaten to death. I had felt death punching me in the face repeatedly that night alone. This stone didn't scare me.

I reached forward and grabbed the stone with both hands, braced for the pain.

I wasn't nearly braced enough.

If you've been burned by flame or by steam, you have a small idea of what it's like to be burned alive. Just imagine the seconds of pain only without end. If you've been punched, you have a small idea of being beaten to death. Imagine the blows keep coming until you stop moving.

The point is that it is easy to imagine what pain is like if you've felt a similar type.

If you've broken a bone, imagine every bone being crushed at the same time. If you've been hit in the head or broken a rib, imagine them being kicked in one by one. Or the sense of taking a hit to the head, just how disorienting that can be. Or accidents with sharp objects slicing the flesh.

This was all worse.

I felt the pressure of my hands ripped with power tools. My fingers crushed by hammers. Being set on fire. Being burned by endless steam. Every bone in my body broke. Every joint shattered and dislocated. My back was set on fire. I was sexually assaulted with and without foreign objects. I was whipped, stripped, hung, crucified, gassed, strangled, shot, and inflicted with every manner of torture that could be devised over thirty years in a torture chamber, a war zone, and in a city where hundreds tried to provoke a reaction of despair and pain.

And I felt every bit of pain and trauma and despair from decades in a matter of seconds.

The pain laid me out so badly I dropped to the floor—but it was over so fast I caught myself before I could hit the marble. *Help.*

Kozbar chuffed. "You're still alive."

Hidden by my doubled over body, I reached into my suit jacket and touched my cell phone.

I looked up and met Kozbar's eyes. I smiled at him with a wolfish grin. "My turn."

I will note here for convenience sake that it did *not* take me two hours to walk from the cafe to Toynbee Tower. It took that long for me to call home, talk to my former partner, and confirm his exact recipe for a useful chemical mixture... *then* I had every altar boy, deacon, and volunteer at the Westminster Cathedral to assemble aluminum tape, iron oxide and magnesium together in the right formula ... then they delivered it. After that, it took what felt like *forever* for me to levitate up the side of Toynbee Tower, smelling my way to the right floor, and placing the thermite charges against all of the office windows, all without being seen.

And it took only seconds for the signal from my cell phone to set off all of the thermite charges.

Every window—two walls of the room—lit up in a massive, exaggerated fireball.

I grabbed the gun in my jacket and shot to my feet in one smooth movement. I whipped the gun out and across Kozbar's face as I jumped up. The pistol-whipping rocked his head back, and I added insult to injury by kicking him away.

With my left hand, I smacked Fowler in the face with the Soul Stone. He fell back, screaming in pain. Then I opened fire with my pistol, shooting out the lights in the ceiling.

The jihadists around us were already distracted with the windows turning into a giant fireball. Those who did see my move couldn't risk opening fire without hitting at least one of their employers. By the time everyone else turned their attention to us, I had shot out all the lights, leaving the only light in the room coming from the wall of fire trying to get into the building.

Then the windows finally shattered under the stress, opening up the chamber to the high winds of being over 400 feet in the air, as well as covering the jihadists in a blanket of broken glass.

Meanwhile, I was running for my life, out of the chamber, into the massive marble hallway, and heading for the elevator.

The elevator doors opened when I was halfway down the hall. The elevator was filled with security guards armed with batons and guns.

I didn't hesitate and tacked right into the first door I saw—it was the stairwell.

I narrowly missed a lighting bolt thrown my direction. It cut through the first guard in the elevator and made the elevator explode.

Then a *second* explosion rocked the building. One of my thermite charges had ignited some of the internal writing of the building and caught a gas main.

All of the lights went black, casting everything into utter darkness...

Except for the fireball coming from the landing below me. One guard leaped through the flames, rolled to put out his uniform, then came up, aiming at me with his MP5.

I tacked left and shot up the staircase as the bullets rang out behind me.

Biraq, the lightning thrower, kicked open the stairway door and nearly walked into the gunfire. He cursed the guard and sent a casual lightning bolt back at him, killing him immediately.

I started up the second set of stairs when the next explosion rocked the building so hard, it threw me into the wall. I bounced against it and caught myself before I started bouncing back down the stairs. The Soul Stone was in the crook of my left arm like it was a football, and I was going to score the touchdown of the game. I kept running for the door of the next level when the door itself exploded open in a massive fireball. I swung around and kept running up. A girder came down out of the ceiling and swung for my head. I dove underneath it, crashing on the next landing above me.

At the next floor up, I crashed into the door with my shoulder, expecting it to open. It bounced me back and wrenched my shoulder. I reared back with a kick and smashed through it. I turned left, into the hallway, and a group of armed guards was coming down the hall for me.

The wall beside them exploded, ripping them apart.

Crap. I think the whole place is coming down? What the hell did I set off?

The ceiling collapsed, blocking my path.

A lightning bolt sizzled past my head, and I ran straight for the fire. Before I had to consider running through the flames, the wall that had exploded was relatively clear of debris. I dove through it.

I had to catch myself before I slid down a bunch of roof tiles.

Roof tiles?

I took a moment to look around. There was still a wall of glass around the building, so I was still inside Toynbee Tower. But I was standing on another structure. Another building. They had moved what looked like a temple into the tower. I felt the stonework. It was older, not modern. They had taken an original, older building, and moved it, brick by brick, into the tower. They had wired it into the rest of the building's utility systems, giving it power and light ... and connecting them to the gas mains.

I hunched down and scrambled along the roof tiles, cornering around as the wall exploded behind me, and more explosions came from below. The roof skirt I was on dead-ended in a wall. I pocketed the Soul Stone and leaped up to the next level up—I couldn't even tell if God levitated me or not, and I wasn't going to stop to ask questions now.

I grabbed a window ledge and worked my way over, hand over hand, and swung myself to the next window over. There was a bit of ledge sticking out, something for me to grab onto—a balcony that ran around the building? I reached up to grab hold when the roar of flames and screaming rushed at me. I pulled my hand back from the ledge when a man on fire flailed and roared as he went over the edge, plummeting to his death. I pulled myself up and charged along the wooden balcony. I ran along the balcony, and it led to a wrecked wall, leading to a hallway on fire.

I turned left, heading for the side of the building away from the exploded elevator and the fiery stairwell. I figured it didn't matter as long as I could get to a window. The hallway ended in a blind corner, and I wheeled around it.

I crashed into a group of three guards. I clothes-lined one as I collided into them, sending him straight to the ground. I whipped the arm around the neck of the second guard and dragged him to the ground between him and number three. I rolled around with guard number two, cutting out the legs out from under the third. I cranked number two's neck with a *crack*. I scrambled to my feet at the same time that the third got to his feet. I leaped over the second and drove a flying knee into the third.

I swept down, picked up one of their MP5s, and pressed on, nearly running onto one of the random furniture items left—first a table, then a wardrobe. I noticed that the flames had not yet reached this area, though the smoke started to leak in.

Two guards popped out down the hallway and fired. I ducked back behind the wardrobe. It was sturdy enough to endure the gunfire. I slid down into a crouch, but I couldn't wait long. The fire was behind me and perhaps also Biraq.

I peeked out around the corner and fired my MP5 at one guard, killing him. He fell back, but the other one had a bulletproof metal shield. He kept coming. He kept firing. He kept coming. Step by step. He'd fire every so often to keep my head down.

I waited until he was so close, I felt the footsteps in the floor as he took a step.

I burst forward, throwing myself across the floor in front of his shield—but my upper body could aim around it. I pressed the MP5 into his side and pulled the trigger, shredding his insides. He didn't even have time to scream.

I rose, charged down the hallway and swept up another MP5. I kept going, even though the way was made more difficult with flaming wooden beams. They had fallen halfway down the hallway, all on fire. I threw myself on the floor and bear-crawled underneath them. I came up and half the ceiling above was torn away. I could see an open window, plain as day. It had been shattered by ...

something. It was only a few more floors up. I could make it if I ran.

The flaming beams behind me exploded with lightning bolts. I whirled and fired, causing Biraq to fall back.

But Shifa kept coming, screaming and laughing like a maniac. I fired for his face, drilling the bullets through his head. No matter how fast he could heal, he wouldn't recover from that in a hurry.

The building shook with another explosion, and I felt the time getting away from me.

Levitation, please, God. Levitation, please, God. Levitation, please, God. Levitation, please, God, I frantically prayed as I leaped for a handhold I saw in the ruined stonework.

I fell back to the wooden planks.

A lightning bolt sizzled over my head where I would have been had I not fallen back. *Well timed, Lord.*

I turned and ran down the hall as the floor caught fire. Biraq took almost no notice as he threw more and more lightning my way— thankfully, as his bolts came faster and more frantic, his aim suffered.

Then a bolt exploded behind me, sending me in the air, crashing onto the floor.

Then the floor gave out from under me.

I reached out and grabbed the floor ahead of me, sending the MP5 clattering to the wood.

"End of the line, infidel."

I looked up and behind me. On the edge of the floor behind me was Biraq, lightning flickering from his eyes and between his fingers.

I was a perfect target.

Then an explosion of fire from behind him ignited Biraq and sent him flying. I ducked my head for fear that he would land on me. He didn't. He fell into the gaping chasm below me—other floors in the building had even given away. The entire building was going to go.

Then Biraq caught my pants leg.

Biraq's weight pulled me down. My fingers slipped between two of the planks of the floor ahead of me, and I jerked myself forward.

Biraq pulled himself up over my body, still on fire. I wouldn't be able to pull up the both of us. I looked down, pulled up one leg, and kicked him in the face. He wouldn't let go, the adrenaline was giving him deranged strength before the end. He made it up to my belt, even though his back and his hair were on fire. He scrambled up my body until I felt his breath on my neck.

I let go with my left hand and drove my elbow into Biraq's face. The blow disoriented him. I struck him once, twice more. Then I heaved forward, grabbed the MP5, and drove the butt of the gun into his forehead.

I shattered the flake of obsidian under his skin.

Suddenly, Biraq's lightning eyes flickered. and his body seized as the electricity he had stored cooked him from the inside out. He screamed in sudden agony that not even being on fire had invoked.

Biraq let go of me and fell, screaming, into the fiery abyss.

I pulled myself up and charged forward. The wall ahead of me led up to the next level. I charged at the wall, kicked up it, and got the height I needed to get a finger hold up. I looked around, and there was a broken ramp going up further still. I thought it was a really stupid idea to keep heading up—until I looked down and saw the flames below, coming to get me.

I ran up the wooden ramp. An explosion of flame fountained up through the ramp, ripping it to pieces right in front of me. Torrents of orange molten metal flowed toward me.

Levitation, please, God, I thought and ran harder, leaping off the edge of the broken ramp and through the flames.

I was certain I was in the air a little longer than I should have been as I came crashing down to the ramp at the other end. I circled around the edge of the temple, going further up. I kicked through the next door.

Then I fell, slamming into the floor below.

I looked up. The walls were on fire. The room I had been walking into didn't have a floor anymore. The floor I was on was only 20 by 10 feet, for a fifty-by-fifty room. Fire had eaten away at the rest of it. I looked down over the edge of the little platform I had left. There weren't any floors below that either. I looked up at a retrofitted wooden staircase that was about twenty, maybe thirty feet away. The wall next to it was on fire, but the stairs weren't in flames Yet.

I backed up for a running start—*Best not to test the Lord thy God by making Him do all the work*—and ran for the edge of the platform. I leaped for the stairs.

I missed the wooden railing.

I missed the safety rail underneath it.

I caught the wooden beam that framed the staircase itself. I pulled up, hauling my carcass behind me.

I saw that the only thing left of the stairs weren't stairs—just the railing. Everything else had burned away, and the railing itself crea- ked, slowly giving way.

I ran along the railing like a balance beam from Hell, only the floor really was on fire. And the walls. And the ceiling. The ceiling glowed with amber light, ready to give way as well.

God, please, levitation, I thought as I ran along the balance beam from Hell. There was a crate suspended from the ceiling. It was fifteen feet tall with several reinforced boards horizontally across its side.

As I neared the edge of the beam, I started a new prayer—to Saint Joseph of Cupertino, patron Saint of Pilots.

Dear ecstatic Conventual Saint who patiently bore calumnies—

I leaped for the crate as flames chased after it.

—your secret was Christ the crucified Savior.

I grabbed the bottom border of the crate. The flames licked at my heels—

Who said: "When I will be lifted up, I will draw all people to myself."

I used the space between the boards to climb up. I hauled myself up two boards at a time, one after another, hefting my weight.

By the time I was halfway up the crate, I noticed the massive label burned into the wood: DANGER: EXPLOSIVES.

I tried to move faster, even though I was already at top speed.

You were always spiritually lifted up, I prayed.

By the time my hands clamped down on the top of the crate, the flames below licked at my shoes so much I felt them smoking.

I pulled my feet up, swung them over the edge, and clambered up. I made it to my feet in time to see that the rope suspending the crate in the air was already on fire—both above me and below me.

Which meant the crate below me was already on fire.

I continued. *Give aviators courage and protection—*

On the other side of the crate was the broken out window. The ropes were burning away.

—and may they always keep in mind your greatly uplifting example.

I ran forward, covering the top of the crate in two leaping strides.

The rope broke.

I leaped.

Amen.

18

WING AND A PRAYER

I missed the window ledge.

I missed the mark by about five feet.

I went through the *center* of the open window.

I spread my arms as though in a swan dive and entered free fall.

All I could think as I fell was simple: the Soul Stone was away from Fowler and Toynbee and Kozbar. Their reign of terror was over. Let them go back to backyard explosives. They were stopped.

Thank you, God. They lost.

I dropped about twenty stories before my wind speed had hit terminal velocity, then I nosed up. The levitation was taking me for a ride, and I didn't fight it. I flew in... and kept flying. I closed my eyes, enjoying the wind on my face. There was no windburn. There was no loss of oxygen. There was just me and God, and a demonic rock.

I looked over my shoulder at Toynbee Tower. The entire top twenty floors were a mass of flame and smoke. It was impossible that anything could have survived that. Granted, the three big names in this battle had been twenty floors *below* the inferno. They could have escaped. But they didn't have the Soul Stone.

And all I could think of was Psalm 30: *I praise you, Lord, for you raised me up and did not let my enemies rejoice over me. O Lord, my God, I cried out to you for help and you healed me. Lord, you brought my soul up from Sheol; you let me live, from going down to the pit.*

You could guess that being raised up was very much on my mind.

As I started to lose altitude, I opened my eyes. I was back in London, at the very edge of the city. I blinked, taken aback. I didn't understand what happened. Why not take me all the way back in?

The answer came to me quickly—London was the home of the CCTV. They had more security cameras on hand than a mall during the Christmas season. It wouldn't do to have me flying on film.

I started walking for the center of the city. Unfortunately, the adrenaline was wearing off, and I felt exhausted.

"Tommy?"

I looked over. It took me a moment to recognize them. They were the first homeless I saved with Pearson before we entered the museum.

"Jillian? Robert?"

They both smiled at me quizzically, looking me up and down. Robert asked, "Good God, man, where did you come from? You look half-roasted."

I looked down at my clothes. I must have smelled like smoke because I looked like an ashtray. "Just a little."

"Where are you trying to get to?"

"Westminster Cathedral."

Robert and Jillian exchanged a look and nodded. "Come on," she said. "We'll get you there."

"Thanks."

Robert and Jillian got me back to the Cathedral without a problem. I suggested they leave by the back way—if we were being followed by anyone, I didn't want them caught in the crossfire. Though I didn't even think that Kozbar's Jihadists could come after me that fast ... but then, if he was in a car within five minutes of the lights going out in the chamber, he could have been back to London before I even got out of the building... if he were speeding. My airspeed was low enough that I didn't die, and I didn't look at my watch along the way. I knew it was night by the time I arrived—the cloud cover had finally departed. The moon and stars shone through. The darkness must have receded entirely into the stone in my jacket pocket.

I dragged myself into the Cathedral. It was a glorious cathedral, with marble everywhere. There weren't pews, but there were wooden chairs. The walls and ceilings were dotted with mosaics. The immense marble baptismal font could have served an adult, bent over and crouched in the chamber. The ceiling of the Lady Chapel was a mosaic in gold leaf that looked just a step above the Greek Orthodox variations of the same art style.

I didn't quite crash, but the exhaustion of the last few hours had me slump into a chair in the back row of the church.

I didn't know how long I sat there before Pearson was smacking me lightly in the face. My eyes opened whether they wanted to or not.

Pearson shook me. "Tommy. Wake up. They're outside."

It took me a long moment of looking at him stupidly before my eyes snapped open. "Which one?" I asked. "All of them?" I couldn't imagine Toynbee and Fowler at the head of an army.

Pearson shook his head. "Only Kozbar. But he's brought his friends. All of his friends."

I blinked twice before it sunk in. *All* his friends sounded like the riot that we confronted that morning—*Yikes, was it only this morning?* I thought. That would make it dozens of people.

I took several deep breaths. I tried to shoot for Psalm 28, but the only part that came out was the end: *Blessed be the Lord, who has heard the sound of my pleading. The Lord is my strength and my shield, in whom my heart trusts. I am helped, so my heart rejoices; with my song I praise him. LORD, you are a strength for your people, the saving refuge of your anointed. Save your people, bless your inheritance; pasture and carry them forever!*

"Let's roll."

Pearson helped me to my feet. "Why haven't they broken in already?"

"The doors were locked once the riot started. We've been acting as sanctuary for people in the basement. They could break in, but it would take time, and it would be noisy. The riots died down hours ago. A full assault would end badly for everyone. They may take the stone, but they may not. Either way, they don't want a fuss if they can avoid it."

I smiled evilly. "They can't. Let's go out and have a conversation."

19

IN THE NAME OF THE LORD

"Did you call the cops?" I asked.

"En route. Though the response time may vary."

I stepped out of the church. The Soul Stone was not in my pocket, but back in the last row of the church. I left Pearson behind me. We opened the door, I slipped out, and Pearson closed it as fast as he could.

The problem was not Kozbar. The major problem wasn't even his Jihadi minions behind him... the problem wasn't even his Jihadi Wolverine, Shifa, who was alive and well and not even scorched, despite everything I had done to the sucker.

No. The real problem was the shadow minions. They grew in form and substance out of the shadows of the Jihadists. Even if the cops arrived, and even if the cops arrived on our side, it would still be a bloodbath. The shadows would eat them alive. Literally. I didn't know if the shadows were demons, or just manifestations of Kozbar's will while he had the Soul Stone, but I knew that the Met wouldn't survive an attack.

"Hey, Kozbar. How are you doing?" I asked casually.

Kozbar smiled. "I am doing quite well. You are surprisingly in one piece. My man Shifa tells me that you survived the burning temple.

No one else did. And yet you're in one piece. You are very fortunate. Tell me, did the stone save you? Are you able to wield it?"

I aborted a laugh. "If I had my druthers, I wouldn't pick up that thing if I found it by the side of the road. The only reason I even touched it was to get it away from the Fowlers and you."

Kozbar narrowed his eyes. "You realize that you cannot win against us."

"Wouldn't be the first time." I smiled. "Wouldn't be the first time we kicked your asses with a handful of people, either."

Kozbar growled. "Do you think you can stop us, *American*?"

I looked over his armed men, their shadow creatures with him, and said, simply, "Yippee Kai yay, motherfucker."

Kozbar scoffed, not taking my witty repartee seriously. "Please. You are soft. You are weak. You are pathetic. Your church is diseased."

"Pathetic?" I asked. "Coming from a culture that had to move West to discover indoor plumbing?"

"Your God is *nothing* next to Allah."

"Funny, I thought we were *all people of the book*."

Kozbar dismissed it with a snort. "Good public relations by the Prophet, Blessed Be His Name. If he *said* he would slaughter you like cattle, the rats would have fought harder. But in the end, you will be like those he subjugated. We know that you would not die for your faith."

I flinched, I admit it. A laugh escaped me before I could let it out. My fingernails scratched against the palms of my hands as I could feel where the shadows speared me before devouring me. I could almost hear the thump of the cricket bats bludgeoning me to death.

"Not die for my faith? I've *died* for my faith more times than you can imagine. I've been burned alive, crushed, impaled, bled out, and stabbed. I have scars each time I died. You can't stop the Lord my God, Kozbar. I am merely the vessel."

Kozbar's brow furrowed, uncertain of what I said. He was uncertain if I was serious, I had lost my mind, or both. "Just what do you think you are?"

"Who am I? I am the Winged Hussars. I am the one hundred

eighty-nine in the service of Heaven. I will protect *all* those of God. I will fight you and hold you back, even to the steps to Heaven. For the grace and might of God, you will not step one foot in this church. You have fallen from the one faith, Kozbar, and your fall from grace will pave your path to damnation."

Kozbar took a step back. "You have five minutes to think it over."

I went back into the church and looked the door behind us.

Pearson asked, "How much time?"

"Five minutes." *If we give it up, they use the stone to melt the doors and kill us with it.* "They can't have it. Under any circumstances."

Pearson shook his head. "No. They can't. We should hide it."

I nodded. "I know exactly where it should go."

I stumbled over to the baptismal font. It was full of water. I walked over to the chair and swept up the Soul Stone. The ruby glyphs had stopped humming at long last ... or at least it had grown so faint that they were nearly out entirely.

"Go back to Hell," I told it. I let go.

It splashed in the baptismal font.

It screamed. The holy water in the baptismal font started *boiling*. Fire shot through the water and into the air, dissipating before the flames struck anything important.

But you can bet that I shot back from the baptismal font like a jackrabbit shot up with cocaine.

Roars and screaming came from outside as well, the shadows, and the Jihadists they were attached to, howled in despair and rage. A wind blew through the church like the prelude to a hurricane. The hanging lights swayed. The statues shook where they stood. Chairs slid across the floor. Debris outside clattered against the windows.

The flames then shot out of the font, through the holy water, spilling out like a fountain of fire. It nearly reached the ceiling, then fell back away from the roof and dissipated. The flames twisted and writhed like a jaguar scruffed by a giant, trying to escape its confinement but unable to escape. The flame howled and shrieked, screaming in pain.

After a long moment, the boiling and the flames died down, and I let my heart rate drop a little bit. I took a deep breath, and for the first time noticed that the smell of evil had cleared away. "I guess that's one way to get rid of the sin the Soul Stone has absorbed."

Pearson looked at me like I was far too calm and said, "Indeed." He looked at the font once more, making sure that the surface of holy water was calm once more. He looked away from it, as though nothing had happened, and asked, "By the way, how did you know he'd understand those references?"

I blinked, confused. "What references?"

"If I heard correctly, you cited the last stand of the Papal Guard in 1527, and the Battle of Vienna, where the Winged Hussars swept in and stopped the Sultan's forces from taking the city."

I bit my lip, shrugged, and said, "I'm not entirely certain I was the one doing the talking there."

"Ah. Understood."

Kozbar slammed against the big brass doors with his AK-47. "Your time just ran out, American!"

I looked at my watch. It had not been five minutes. "I think the Jihadi brigade outside knows what we did."

Pearson nodded, then frowned. "I could go outside and bluff them a bit."

I shook my head. "They're going to want what they came for, no matter what. Going outside is pure suicide. They're going to get testy and beat someone to death."

Pearson looked at me, as though he could see what I was thinking. "You're not going out there."

I shrugged. There were any number of tricks that the Lord had granted me over the past year or so. I could bi-locate and riot control them—

And I could die a few more times, wouldn't that be fun?

I could dive bomb them via levitation—*What is "skeet" is Arabic?*

I could even... no, those were the only two ideas I had in mind.

Dear God, if you need me to die here, then I presume it's for a good reason. Let's do this.

I turned. I thought I was going to turn to the door, but I didn't. I turned to the Lady Chapel. I knelt down in the gold-leaf hall and prayed one more time.

Heavenly King, You have given us archangels to assist us during our pilgrimage on earth.

Saint Michael is our protector; I ask him to come to my aid, fight for all my loved ones, and protect us from danger.

Saint Gabriel is a messenger of the Good News; I ask him to help me clearly hear Your voice and to teach me the truth.

Saint Raphael is the healing angel; I ask him to take my need for healing and that of everyone I know, lift it up to Your throne of grace and deliver back to us the gift of recovery.

Help us, O Lord, to realize more fully the reality of the archangels and their desire to serve us.

Holy angels, pray for us. Amen.

I crossed myself, stood, and headed for the door. Pearson stepped in my way, placing his hand on my chest to stop me.

"God the Father of mercies, through the death and resurrection of his Son has reconciled the world to himself and sent the Holy Spirit among us for the forgiveness of sins; through the ministry of the Church may God give you pardon and peace, and I absolve you from your sins in the name of the Father, and of the Son and of the Holy Spirit. Amen."

"Amen."

Pearson met my eye, clapped me on the shoulder, and said, "God be with you."

"If He's left me alone once, I hadn't noticed."

I stepped to the doors. I stopped before opening them and called out, "Back off. I'm coming out. I see anyone within thirty feet of the door, you're not getting anything from me."

After a few seconds, Kozbar screamed back, "Done."

Pearson unlocked the door and pushed it open. I slipped between the doors and helped Pearson close it. The jihadists were still there, but the shadow creatures weren't.

I stuck my hands in my pockets. *Lord, now would be a good time to bi-locate, so I can flank them.* "Kozbar."

"Nolan. Where is the stone?"

"It's gone," I said, telling only a half-truth. "It didn't react well to holiness."

Kozbar growled. "No... NO!" he roared. He reached behind him for the back of his belt and came back with a machete. "I will *cut* the Soul Stone out of you, infidel, and feed you your heart."

I raised both hands up and waved him on. I wanted him angry and stupid, so I came up with the worst insults I could think of. "Come and get me, dog. When I'm done, I will feed your corpse to pigs."

Kozbar roared as he rushed me.

But then, so did all the others.

I braced one foot behind me and braced for impact.

I blinked.

Suddenly, there were three men in front of me, standing between the crowd and me. Even Kozbar skidded to a stop in front of them.

Kozbar looked them up and down. The three men were strangely dressed. One wore an American army uniform and hat, complete with general's stars. The one to his left wore medical scrubs. The one on the right wore a simple suit and tie.

"Who are you?" Kozbar asked.

"Requested reinforcements," said the army man. His voice was gruff and bored, as though Kozbar were simply Tuesday for him.

Kozbar sneered. He stabbed forward with the weapon, pointing at me between two of the "reinforcements." He demanded, "Then give him to me. And me alone. I promise to kill him personally. You want fair fights, right?"

The one in scrubs stepped back and grabbed my shoulder, holding me back. "Sure. He's gotten his ass kicked all over the place, died five times, fought down a riot, and escaped an exploding building the hard way, while you get to go after him after ... walking down some stairs and driving here?"

The army man said, "You get one chance."

Kozbar sneered. "My God is on my side. Nothing more or less will stop me."

The army man's head tilted just slightly to one side. "About that..."

Kozbar lunged with the knife.

The army man smacked Kozbar across the face and sent him flying.

Scrubs said, "Go back inside, Tommy. We got this."

I blinked hard, confused. "I missed a step. Who are you?"

He smiled at me benevolently. "You asked for us directly. You know who we are. You're just too exhausted to think about it." He reached over, grabbed the door, opened it—*Wasn't it locked a moment ago?*—and ushered me inside, closing the door behind me.

The moment the door closed, every light in the church glowed brightly as the screaming started and the laser light show began. I grabbed the door to push it open—and it was locked, even though I had just walked through the open doors.

Pearson looked up from his seat in one of the chairs. "What are you doing back? How did you get in? And – —what is *that*?"

It took me a long moment. So long that the screaming, the glowing, and the light show all faded away. But the fog had lifted from my brain, as had all of the exhaustion.

Before I had gone out, I prayed to a healer, a warrior, and a messenger. Then a man in scrubs, a uniform, and a suit show up.

"The reinforcements," I said plainly. "If you don't mind, I think I'm going to say some prayers and go to bed."

Pearson unlocked the door and looked outside. Kozbar was gone. His Jihadists were gone.

But there was the faint smell of sulfur.

20

STONY PATH

A fter mass the next morning, Pearson and I ate breakfast by ourselves in the rectory. Everyone else had spent the day cleaning up the city after the riot. There were plenty of riot refugees in the basement for the regular workers at the Cathedral.

Pearson brought the full English breakfast to the table for both of us. "So, what's on the agenda today? Back off to Rome?"

I dug into the two-pound plate of food. After running around the city all day and night, being beaten and then miraculously healed the night before, all without eating, I was ravenous. I ate a few forkfuls, thinking it over. I shook my head. "I can't leave yet. Not until the Soul Stone is destroyed."

Pearson blinked, taken aback. "Why try? Bring it back to Rome, see what happens?"

I looked at Pearson cynically. "Let me get this straight; you expect me to get through a major transportation checkpoint—like the Chunnel, or Heathrow—with a diamond larger than my fist, which happens to mysteriously bear heavy similarities to a well-known artifact stolen from the British Museum. Meanwhile, I can only suppose that the Fowlers are going to have a full-court press on getting me strung up by the cops. Getting me out of the country with Fowler and

Toynbee pushing the cops for my head? I can't see that happening. Not to mention that Toynbee Tower was largely blown up as we checked out last night. Once the story about the riot cycles down, you can be certain that Toynbee and Fowler are going to push a narrative in the news cycle that marks me as a terrorist. Who knows, if they own enough newspapers and have enough friends in the national press, they may be able to blame me for the riot last night, too. No. If anything is going to happen, we either need to get Fowler and Toynbee arrested, or destroy the Soul Stone. I can take being arrested. I can't take going through all of this all over again because we dropped the ball."

Pearson nodded, absorbing everything I told him. While he thought, I ate quickly. I didn't want the food to get cold in case he asked me another question.

I was right. The next question he asked was going to take time.

"What happened last night?" Pearson asked.

I explained. Twice. He followed along better the second time, then repeated it back to me, just to be clear.

After a long, thoughtful silence—by Pearson, I was just hungry—he shrugged. "First time angels popped out of the sky for you?"

"In part because I didn't even know I was asking." I frowned. I tried not to think about it the night before, largely because I wanted to get to sleep and be done with it. "Angels? Why, though? I didn't directly ask. I didn't even know that was a request I could submit in the file form of God's rules and regulations. Nor did I know that they would show up. Heck, I'm surprised I got one. I got three." I reached for the cup of tea, then stopped and looked at Pearson. "In fact, when was the last time the Vatican saw an angel pop out of the sky? It's not like they showed up for me before."

"In answer to your latter, implied question, it's more than likely that there wasn't another option for you last night," Pearson answered. "And you've handled the demonic before. You had other options. But bi-locating in your condition while you were heavily battered? It's unlikely that it would have gone well."

I waited to swallow my current mouthful. "How about my actual question? When was the last time this happened? Battle of Britain?"

"More often than you'd think." Pearson frowned. "The demonic is rising, Tommy."

I said nothing, letting him fill in the silence. It was a tactic that worked for interrogations. I was less interested in interrogating him than I was in eating. Fasting was fine, fasting during a running battle with Jihadists, shadows, and police officers, all before climbing a towering inferno? That was a little much.

Pearson paused for a long, long moment. "You're not the only one who's been fighting the darkness, Detective Nolan. You're not alone. Never forget that part. Demons are on the rise. Darkness is routinely praised in the newspapers. Your own Mayor was getting away with only mildly exaggerated forms of coercion of everyday people than the regular political class. And he was pure evil. The cult you fought. That was also evil, but it was one of the most monied, powerful and connected organizations in a city that runs on money, power, and connections. And they're considered 'respected.' Just imagine what it'll be like a few years from now. We already have academics suggesting we snuff granny if she walks funny. In the UK, our National Health Service would rather let children die than allow them to go anywhere else on the continent and get treatment. In America, there would be civilians with guns ready to rescue the child and burn the NHS on the way out. Here? The populous has largely forgotten about it already."

I frowned, my plate cleaned. I would mull over this later. The problems of the world were too big for me right now, especially before coffee.

I stood. "Come on, we need to get to work on the Soul Stone before something else goes wrong. Scotland Yard should be busy the day after a race riot. But let's not be *too* easy to find."

The morning was spent working on the easy ways of cracking the Soul Stone. We didn't know why it looked like a diamond, but even if it had changed from obsidian to diamond, he wouldn't be an obstacle. Diamonds could be cut. At the right angle, diamonds could break.

First, it occurred to me that no one had actually tried to *break* the Soul Stone. The archaeologists wanted to collect a sample off of it to test it for aging. They couldn't do that while being delicate. Kozbar and the Fowlers wanted a few flakes for the personal use of their own minions. Once their minions had a flake of the gem embedded in their flesh, the pieces of the stone could be charged with the personal hatreds and negative emotions of the wielder and the darkness around them.

No one had tried to simply hit the damn thing with a hammer. So that was the first thing I did. I placed the Soul Stone on the floor of the basement in the Cathedral, reared back with a claw hammer, and slammed down on it.

The heavy wooden handle *cracked*. The handle broke so that a few wood fibers barely held on as the handle bent into a right angle.

I frowned. "Okay. Maybe not."

The next step was a nail gun. That was a simple trip to another side of the church basement. The short version is that the Vatican owes Westminster Cathedral a new nail gun.

One of the folks who had come to hide in the Cathedral basement during the riot last night walked in on us doing this and wondered what we were doing. When we explained, he took us over to one side of the basement and slightly opened his jacket. In his belt was the handle of a German Luger. He hid it away again, looking around the empty basement as though someone was going to take it away from him. It had been a souvenir from World War Two and a family heirloom. It was the sort of gun that shot through several people at once, and would we like to borrow it?

We were prepared for the test firing. We found a thick wooden box and put the Soul Stone inside. Both the gun's owner and Father Pearson left the basement to protect against ricochets. I whipped up some ear protection. (No, I wasn't going to fire a Luger in an enclosed space.) I fired three careful rounds into the Soul Stone from thirty feet away.

After the third bullet, I stopped firing. The Soul Stone hadn't even chipped. But the bullets had shattered, turning into shrapnel and perforating the wooden box more than a block of Swiss cheese.

We thanked Father Laroche from the next parish over and handed him his Luger back.

The next step was to take the Soul Stone out into the city. We went out the back way, just to make certain that Inspector Shaw and the police weren't out looking for us. We weren't worried about the CCTV cameras since they had been installed all over the city and the crime rate hadn't dropped.

The city was quiet after the race riot. You could call it subdued. The traffic was cut by a quarter. The traffic jams still popped up, but no one was in a real rush to go anywhere or brutalize anybody. The occasional shouts were at kids and teenagers with their heads in their phone, telling them to watch where they were going. But no one had the heart for violent road rage. Cabbies went about their business in silence. Everyone obeyed the laws and the traffic lights out of mechanical habit because they didn't have the energy for timed bursts of speed or aggressive driving through a knot of traffic. The M25 around London was knotted, and no one even honked their horn.

The city was muted, but the sun was shining. For the first time, I went out in sunlight and could feel it on my face. The shadows had gone.

We visited a construction site and asked to borrow one of their diamond-tipped drills. Thankfully, those are relatively cheap, so we didn't really cost the foreman anything. Five minutes under a blow torch did nothing to it, either.

We went down to a dark alley for a meet Pearson had arranged. A shadowy man in black pulled up, did a brush-pass with Pearson, and moved on. It happened so fast, I was tempted to ask if Pearson had been pick-pocketed. Pearson looked at me, shook his head and moved along. We went down to the Thames River, near the reconstructed Globe Theater, and Pearson showed me what the meet was about. He opened his jacket and showed me a coil of bright yellow cord with diagonal stripes wrapped around it every few inches.

I arched a brow. "Det cord?"

Pearson nodded.

"Which parish are you from again?" I asked.

Pearson smiled and said nothing.

I rolled my eyes. "Okay. *Be* cryptic."

We wrapped the det cord around the Soul Stone. It was a solid cocoon. We laid it in a concrete planter on the banks of the Thames. We walked a good distance away, behind shelter, checked the area was empty—no one wanted to run out the day after a race riot—and detonated the explosive. The planter exploded as though it was a window sill flower pot hit with a baseball.

Pearson and I went over to the planter.

The Soul Stone didn't even lose its shine. It was still clearer than glass. Since it looked like a diamond now, it would have shown a scratch.

Pearson glared at it. "Do we need Mount Doom to destroy this lousy thing?"

"We take it back to the Cathedral," I said, "and you start praying over it. If Holy Water purged the crap out of it, maybe we can pray it to death."

Pearson shook his head. "Trust me, I did that last night after you went to bed. It didn't work."

As this point, you may have asked yourself, Why not use the Stone Soul to destroy itself? It was a perfectly reasonable question. Kozbar's people used the Soul Stone to collect the flakes they used. Why *not* use the Soul Stone against itself? The short answer is that I wasn't going to try using the Soul Stone at all, never mind trying to turn it on itself. Especially since I had no idea if the stone itself was aware. If it had any concept of how to defend itself, it had the tools. My first touch of the stone had proven that. I didn't want to think of what it would do to me if I tried to turn it on itself.

My question was why the angels hadn't taken it away with them.

We sulked back to the cathedral, defeated.

I opened the door of the cathedral and was hit with a smell of sin and corruption that I hadn't detected since last night after we had dropped the Soul Stone in the baptismal font.

Pearson saw my reaction and walked me over to the wall so I could get a grip. He went back and closed the door. The Cathedral was empty except for me, Pearson, and ... *who else?*

Footsteps echoed from the Lady Chapel. We turned. The footsteps were from army boots. They were black, to match the slacks. He wore a gray London Fog raincoat. He even wore his fedora inside.

"I've been waiting for you gentlemen," Inspector Aaron Shaw said.

21

HEART OF STONE

Aaron Shaw stepped forward calmly and casually, as though he hadn't tried to run Pearson and me down like dogs the other day.

"So happy to see you two survived being out in the riot yesterday," he said calmly, his raspy voice coming out like a natural growl, no matter how genial he tried to sound. His hands were in his pockets. "Congratulations. But I'm afraid that you'll both have to go to jail."

"Charges?" Pearson asked.

Shaw gave a little smile. "Terrorism. Destruction of property. Attempted murder of Lord Fowler and Dame Toynbee. Theft of the Soul Stone from the museum. You have it, don't you?"

I shrugged. "Does it matter? You're going to frame us for all of it."

Shaw's brows arched just a little. He cocked his head. His smile widened just a little, the smile boasting *prove it*. "Oh really? What makes you think that?"

"Fowler and Toynbee had no explosives stolen," I told him. I looked at Pearson. He had drifted over to the back row, leaving me closer to the door. "I got a close look at them when they tried to kill me yesterday." I smiled at Shaw as he got closer. He was forty feet away and closing. "I suspect you're not nearly as much of an idiot as you pretend to be. You could have found them with a minute's worth of investigation. I don't think you let anger cloud your judgment ... at least not about this."

Shaw's step paused a moment, but only for a beat. He kept closing, slowly. "Then where is my judgment clouded?"

I shrugged. The next step was a guess, but given what the Fowler's believed, Shaw was a stereotype. "Your bearing is stiff and military." I looked at his pockets. "But the military teaches you to never stick your hands in your pockets. So you have a weapon. It's not a gun, but it's heavy. Special Forces knife? I'm thinking ..." I looked him up and down. "SAS? Your attitude at the precinct says you hate Americans. Working with Fowler and Toynbee means you hate Catholics. Former SAS means you hate the Irish. So an Irish Catholic New York cop must be pushing all of your buttons. Am I close, or would you like to give me a few guesses?"

Shaw's smile faded, and his eyes became hooded. He drew the knife out of his pocket, looking over both me and Pearson. "No. That was quite enough for now." He stopped twenty feet away from me and Pearson, the tip of the triangle. "I'll take the stone now." Shaw glared. "You have it in your pocket. Don't you? That isn't a gun bulging in your jacket."

I smiled. "You're just going to kill us anyway. Molon Labe, sucker." *Come and get it.*

He grinned. "Good. I hoped you would say that."

Shaw stalked toward us but paused, unsure of who to attack first. His eyes flicked to me as the obvious target. I was bigger than Pearson, and a cop, the obvious threat.

Pearson, however, was a spy, and sneaky, and didn't hesitate to grab a chair from the back row and hurl it at Shaw. It smashed across the back of Shaw's head. Shaw staggered closer to me and unsteadily turned to Pearson.

I burst forward and hammered my fist behind Shaw's right ear. Shaw rocked back, teetering off to the side. Shaw whirled, slashing at me with the knife. He caught my coat.

His knife bounced off of the Soul Stone.

Shaw smiled crookedly and stepped forward, slashing again with the knife. I tried to dodge, but he still caught my jacket, again clinking off of the Soul Stone.

Pearson ran up behind him with another chair and smashed it over Shaw's head.

Shaw staggered forward, and I cuffed his ear, bouncing him off of the marble wall.

Then the Soul Stone slipped out through the hole in my pocket created by Shaw's knife work. Shaw darted forward, swept up the Soul Stone, and rolled away from us. He came up to his feet in front of the doors.

Shaw grinned. "You see, I didn't need to kill you two. I just needed the stone. Fowler and Toynbee have enough political clout and muscle in this country to see that both of you either spend the rest of your lives in jail or just go six feet under."

I glowered at him. "I will pray for your redemption, Shaw. But frankly, as far as I'm concerned, you can just go to Hell."

Shaw laughed. "Nice one, American. I'll see you there."

The Soul Stone pulsed with a bright white light in Shaw's hand. His hand closed around it firmly, as though he were afraid that it would get away. It glowed brightly, making it and him hard to look at. It pulsed faster and faster, and Shaw looked directly into the light, unable to look away. His eyes widened in terror as the stone pulsed so fast it looked like a strobe light. I couldn't even look at it.

Shaw screamed three seconds before he burst into flames. His knife went flying as he tried to put himself out. He patted at the flames, trying to keep them down, but every one he put out, three more would ignite. His hair caught fire. The back of his jacket was a curtain of flame. The fire extinguisher was behind him. I whipped off my overcoat and threw it on him in an attempt to smother the flame.

The flames burst white hot through my overcoat. The explosion knocked me back and sent me sliding back along the marble floor.

The flames went up in a flash that consumed both Shaw and my coat.

The Soul Stone hit the floor with a *clink*.

Pearson rushed to my side and grabbed my arm to pull me up. "I guess he took you literally."

I gave an involuntary laugh. "I guess so. Let's get the rock and get out of here before—"

A hand reached through the cathedral doors and grabbed the Soul Stone.

Lord Fowler stepped into the cathedral. His umbrella hung over his left arm, his hat resting in the crook of his elbow. He was elegantly dressed in a black silk suit. Lady Polly Toynbee walked in right behind him.

Toynbee held a pistol. Fowler placed the Soul Stone in his left hand and grabbed his umbrella. One button press released the umbrella, revealing the sword within.

"Good day," Fowler said. "So happy we could catch you."

I grimaced. "Nice. So glad you didn't lose all your suits in the fire."

His expression darkened. "You will pay for all you destroyed, Inspector."

"Hard to replace a temple. What was all that about?"

"Oh, another artifact brought to us by our extraterrestrial visitors. We had it moved to London brick by brick and stone by stone. Now do step away," Fowler joyfully requested. "It would be terrible if we had to murder you both *here*. I think you'd both much rather enjoy a sporting chance as you try to leave the country."

I looked at the Soul Stone in Fowler's hand. It was still as clear as a diamond. Not even being held by Shaw or Fowler could get it to darken.

But for the first time, I noticed that the silver glyphs pulsed faintly with light.

Fowler talked. I didn't hear a single word he said. There were vague threats about taking the stone, killing Pearson and me, and then destroying the religious of London, one by one if they had to. Perhaps they would even take over the British Empire. Fowler was, after all, 128th in line to the British throne (Seriously, he counted?). With the stone, there would be no end to their power, blah blah blah, yadda yadda yadda. It was all James Bond villain monologue with a hint of Saturday morning cartoon special.

I interrupted with, "Have you actually *used* the stone?"

Fowler arched a brow. He looked annoyed that I would be so rude as to interrupt him. "Of course not. This is the first time I've ever held it outside of the museum. Why do you ask, dear boy?"

"Because it takes a strong will to use the stone. Say what you like about Jihadists—misogynistic, barbaric, violent, irrational, downright uncivil. But they have something you lack. They have conviction. Even they have the courage of their convictions. What do you have, Fowler? You believe in nothing. You couldn't even use the stone to kill *us*, never mind use it to destroy London."

Fowler's normally pleasant expression faded. His eyes became hooded, like a viper's. "Oh really?" he drolled, his voice deep and cavernous.

I nodded and stepped forward. "Really. You believe in nothing. You think the entire world is materialism and nothing but the physical." I kept coming, ignoring Toynbee's gun and the sword. "You have no imagination. You can't imagine what right and wrong and justice look like. You're holding a rock that sucks in sin and death and your brain can't *imagine* anything better than aliens!"

I stepped up to his sword point. The tip of it touched my shirt button. I sneered. "You couldn't use that stone if your life depended on it."

"Indeed." He lowered the sword but raised the stone. "Let's see what happens when a superior intellect controls one of the greatest powers of all time."

Fowler stared at me, concentrating his way to a deadly blast. I watched as he hated me with as much energy as he could muster. Despite all of his bantering, all his pretty little speeches, all he amounted to was pure hatred. I met his eyes, and I didn't blink.

His entire focus was set on me. His teeth clenched as though he was in the middle of the most strenuous labor of his life.

"Help. Me. Polly," Fowler demanded, his voice strained.

Lady Toynbee switched hands with the pistol and reached over to grab the Soul Stone.

I reached forward and laid the very tips of my fingers on the forward tip of the stone. "I forgive you both. Don't destroy yourselves. You can't do this."

Fowler growled, an angry, feral animal. "Damn you, Nolan. Damn you. And your priest. *And* your church! And your *God*!"

Considering what happened to Shaw, I knew what would happen next. "I'm sorry."

Fowler's eyes widened, infuriated. "How *dare* you think you can apologize to me. You could never atone for your crimes."

"No. I'm sorry for you."

Fowler and Toynbee glared at me as though they could burn me down by glaring hard enough.

The Soul Stone magnified hate, corruption, and sin. But it was in a church. It had been submerged in holy water overnight. It had been prayed over by a combat exorcist. It could magnify corruption and darkness all it liked ... but it couldn't absorb it.

And I wouldn't let it.

Fowler screamed, first in range, then in pain. A flicker of flame started in his mid-chest, then spread. It broadened out in a circle of fire that consumed him.

"Rest in peace," I said gently.

"No! Noooooo!"

The fire flashed out, vaporizing both Fowler and Toynbee.

I caught the Soul Stone before it could hit the ground.

"Well done," Pearson said. "Did you have to kill them?"

I looked over my shoulder at Pearson. "I didn't. I tried to warn them."

"So that wasn't even a bit of reverse psychology?"

I shook my head. "Nope. Sorry. I genuinely tried to save them. They couldn't control the stone, and it magnified everything inside them. And let it fester there. It ate them up."

Pearson nodded, looking over at where they'd been. "And made an ash out of all of them. I see that."

I sighed, considering the next step. "We're still fugitives. Even a bastard like Shaw probably wrote down our names and alleged crimes before coming out to kill us. Now that the lead investigator and the accusers are all dead, you can be sure everyone else on the police force will come after us."

Pearson simply smiled at that. He reached into his blazer pocket and pulled out his cell phone. "These are all cameras now, remember. I think I can talk some sense into the authorities."

22

TEA IN THE TOWER

F ather Pearson had turned over all of his video evidence to the police. And to the media. And streamed it to the Internet. All three sources went out of their way to purge, scrub, and delete it from memory. The police and the government were quite happy to forget that I, or the Soul Stone, even existed. In fact, they went out of their way to be hospitable about it. Some nameless government minister made certain to loan us Fowler's private jet.

Within twenty-four hours after the mysterious deaths of Fowler and his wife, their entire estate was confiscated by the British government for liquidation.

It was all covered up in a very prim, proper, very British fashion.

The day after the incident with Fowler and Toynbee, Pearson took me out to see the Tower of London. I spent some thirty minutes pondering the life and times of my baptismal patron, Thomas More. I then set about ignoring the tower's history of false imprisonment and death and focused on it being a very picturesque spot next to the Thames. We stopped off at the Tower McDonald's (Yes, it's real. You might imagine that none of the people who *worked* at the Tower were very happy about it existing) and grabbed a tea.

Pearson went off to talk with some people who worked there that he knew from "the old days," and left me to my thoughts, looking out at the Thames. It was peaceful, quiet. Aside from the width, it was like every other river. Eyeing it, I couldn't say it was any wider than the Hudson or East rivers. The flow was smooth and peaceful. The wind was gentle and calm...

And then I smelled it. Evil. Not as corrupt as a demon, but certainly as vile as a human being seeped in sin and spiritual sewage.

Before I turned to face it, I heard ... applause. The noise was vigorous and excited. Even joyous.

I turned to face the man who had jockeyed for the number one position in haunting my nightmares. He was tall and lanky. His skin was light brown, a color palate that could pass for anything in the Mediterranean. His smile was big and broad, with teeth so white they could be seen in the dark. He was bald as an egg. Today he wore a tourist board knockoff of kente cloth, swathed in a robe of yellow, with a pattern of red and green.

He laughed with a great, booming, melodious voice, and said, in his Haitian accent, "Congratulations Detective Nolan! On your great success!"

Bokor Baracus, Voodoo necromancer and bane of my existence, bent down his nearly seven-foot height, swept up his coffee mug, and strode over to join me. I stood to one side of a park bench, and he stood at the other.

I looked him up and down. The last time I had seen him, he had been on fire, being burned away by a chemical so complex I didn't ask how it set concrete on fire, as he expelled clouds of toxic acid that melted glass. By the time the fires burned out, there had been nothing left of him. And if there had been, they would have been consumed by the massive fireball of sulfur that fell out of the sky, struck the house, set it on fire, and created a temporary portal to Hell that sucked in Bokor's boss, warlock Mayor Ricardo Hoynes.

But Baracus looked none the worse for wear.

I took a sip from my tea, my eyes never leaving him. "So. Why am I not shooting you?"

Baracus laughed in that booming, melodic voice. "You have no gun. That's why." He shook his head as though I said something a little stupid and very funny. He looked out over the river Thames, sipping his own McDonald's hot cup.

I nodded. That made sense at least. "Then why aren't you summoning a small zombie army to kill me?"

"As though that worked *last* time. Ha!" Baracus grinned with those big white teeth. "Because no one is *paying* me to kill you."

I raised a brow, studying him. Baracus looked at me and sighed. "You seem to misunderstand me, Detective. I am merely a mercenary. I was paid already. Well over a month ago."

I squinted at him, trying to make him focus ... or make myself focus on him. I wasn't entirely clear at the time. "Didn't Alex kill you? Should I even ask how?"

Baracus laughed. "I am a necromancer. Killing me is more difficult than that."

I nodded. I felt stupid for even asking. "If you've been paid, then what are you doing here?"

He shrugged casually, as though he were just in the neighborhood. "Nothing. I merely wanted to congratulate you on your latest victory."

I blinked, confused. "Why?"

Baracus turned to face me now, taking a sip. He studied me for a moment this time. "Detective Nolan, I am *very* much the opposite of you in *every* sense of the word. I do not serve others for the sake of serving. I serve myself, and I work for money. Or favors. Or power. In terms of Heaven and Hell, I am a mercenary who works for Hell. If only because Heaven would not do the things I would want it to do. But in the grand scheme of the battle between good and evil, I want no one to win. If good wins, the source of my power stops, I die and go to Hell. If evil wins ... I am no longer useful, so there is no reason for my Friends on the Other Side to grant me powers. I die, and I go to Hell. Either way, it does not end well for me. Controlling a city? That is fine. It will not end the world. Destroying a city? Again, it is not the end of all."

I tilted my head, thinking it over. *Destroying a city?* "You were involved with the Soul Stone?"

Baracus shrugged. "After a fashion. I was a consultant. They wanted my expertise, and I left. To be honest, I was glad to be rid of them all."

I blinked, taken aback. "They were too evil for you?"

Baracus barked a laugh. "No. There is no such thing as too evil for me. But they did not understand. Kozbar believed he was working for God. The Lord and Lady thought they were dealing with an alien artifact. I told them what I could of the legends and moved along."

I raised one eyebrow. "You didn't translate the glyphs for them?"

Again, a big, exaggerated shrug. "They did not ask. I did not tell them."

I almost smiled. "Your friends on the other side wouldn't object?"

Baracus paused, his own smile fading. "That is a risk I decided to take. Besides, no one would believe me if I told them. Or if they did believe me, they would have thought it would not have applied to them. So the end results would be similar."

I nodded slowly, absorbing just how crafty Baracus had to be to keep alive without getting burned by his friends on the other side. "How about telling me what they mean?"

Baracus's mouth bunched up in one corner in a half smile. "Now now, that would be telling. Besides, Detective, I suspect you've gotten the gist of it already. Especially if I understood what happened to the Lord and Lady, and their pet policeman."

After a fashion, he was correct. "Should I ask where you're going next?"

"No. But you may ask where I've been."

"You were just in New York a few months ago."

"And between New York and London," Baracus corrected, "I was in Germany."

I blinked. He had actually told me. I almost didn't believe him. But then I realized that Fowler and Toynbee had also spent bundles of money bringing "refugees" into Germany as well as London. If they were the same type of refugee, I would be spending time there as well. And he had to be crafty enough to walk a fine line between serving the powers of Hell, but not yet

"Why tell me about it?" I asked him. "Another way to keep Hell from winning?"

Baracus smiled evilly this time, and his eyes narrow. "No. Their last check bounced." He put the cup to his lips and drank deeply. "I will see you around, Detective. One day, you and I will meet again. I look forward to offering you up to my Friends. You will pay a great many debts one day. I might even retire from this life with you as my payment."

"As the kids say, bring it."

Baracus nodded, almost a theatrical bow. "I will. One day. But today is not your day."

BACK IN ROME, Auxiliary Bishop Xavier O'Brien leaned back in his chair and read my report. "Germany, he said?"

I nodded. "It's all there."

XO nodded, reading the report through a cloud of cigarette smoke. "We'll keep an eye on Germany the best we can. If we're lucky, all of those donations from Fowler to refugee causes will make it easy to trace what Baracus was doing there."

"And what about Baracus?" I asked.

"While he's a threat, we're not in the business of assassination. Hunting him down isn't on the agenda. If we can stop him, we can and we will. But if he's just out and about, merely existing, that's another conversation. He's dangerous but not actively trying to destroy the world."

"This week."

XO laughed and coughed on some smoke. "True. This week. But we can only work on one week at a time."

I nodded. "And the Soul Stone?"

"We'll keep it in the basement," XO said. "If we file it away, it'll be safely lost in the backlog of artifacts and documents until long after the two of us are dead and gone. The nice thing everyone forgets is that *secreta* in the "secret" archives means "unsorter," not "hidden" or "secret." We're going to bury it in the thousand years of paperwork. It's the next step to filing it away in a warehouse of crates next to the ark of the covenant. Heck, we only just found the annulment papers filed by Henry VIII a few years ago. At the very least, when they find it again, *I'll* be dust and a few scraps of bone." XO eyed me up and down. "Though if you become one of the incorruptibles, I'll be amused."

I shook my head. I hadn't meant to ask about that, though it was nice that he told me about it. "I meant how does it operate?"

XO gave me a look as though he didn't believe me. "From this report, I think you have a fairly good guess."

"Humor me."

XO looked at me for several long, slow puffs. "You know what Enochian script is, yes?"

"It's a cipher made in the ... what? Late medieval? Early modern period? Usually called the script of the angels?"

XO nodded. "Close enough. Late fifteen hundreds." He put down the report and let out a long, slow stream of smoke into the air, where the top window of his office was open. "You see, we have some of our own specialists and historians. They know *actual* Enochian script, the *real* language of the angels, not that half-assed cipher drawn up by some occultist."

XO moved the pipe to the corner of his mouth and brought the chair down, leaning forward. He reached into his desk drawer and came up with the Soul Stone. He handled it like he would any dust collector from his mantelpiece. He held it towards me, silver-side first, and ran his finger along the glyphs.

"The silver glyphs tell you that 'he who worships God and loves His people will wield this stone in joy for all the days of their life.' " XO turned the stone upside down. "The red glyphs mean that 'those who dwell in sin and—"

"—and live in corruption," I filled in, "shall be destroyed by the stone."

XO looked over the stone at me. I shrugged. "For some reason, it just became really clear to me," I explained.

"Reading in tongues now, too? Gee, you're a fricking Swiss army knife of charisms." He placed the Soul Stone on his towering in-box pile as though it were a paperweight. "So you see, the stone isn't pure evil in and of itself. Nothing pure evil can exist. It doesn't absorb purely vile vibrations of the soul. It's a metaphysical battery. It can be charged with feelings of pain or feelings of love. But as you guessed, it doesn't take an evil person to use it, just someone of *will* to use it. The power itself isn't evil. It's simply power. Like a battery, it can be plugged into a bomb or into a light bulb. Even the Jihadists were able to power their small flecks just with the power of their own rage and hatred."

"But I don't get it," I told him. "Where did the stone come from? The legends say Anubis handed it over?"

XO sighed, leaning on the desk heavily on one elbow. "Remember that history goes back only six thousand years, give or take. Humans themselves have been around for a few million years, also give or take. Even in the 1920s, archaeologists were digging up signs and artifacts that pointed to a monotheistic culture. Even before Abraham. So most people understood that there was one God. Over time, myths developed. Polytheism sprang up as cultures came, collided, and went." He poked the Soul Stone with the butt of his cigarette. "This came from a time when giants walked the Earth. Back when Genesis was current events. The time of vampires and elves, and myths. If you're a fan of *Lord of the Rings*, consider it a Silmaril—a stone of light. In the right hands, anyway."

I paused for a long moment, and we sat there in silence for a long moment. "So I gathered." I shifted in my chair. "So, now what? Do I head out to Germany?"

XO smiled around his cigarette. "And do what? Investigate every random crime until you hit upon the sinister plot? No. Get out of here. Spend time with your family. You've finished the mission. Take a break. I was told you should be having a daughter sometime soon.

Get on the plane before she shows up. Your ticket is waiting for you in your cell."

My face broke out in a wide grin. "Thank you."

XO snorted, smoke coming out of his nostrils. "Don't thank me. You're the one who saved London from becoming a smoking crater. Go forth in peace to love and serve the Lord, or whatever."

I laughed, shot out of the chair, and left. I was going home.

COMING SOON

Come back next month for Crusader, book five of Saint Tommy, NYPD!

If you liked this one – or any of the others – be sure to leave a review on Amazon. And keep us in mind for the upcoming Dragon Awards.

CPSIA information can be obtained
at www.ICGtesting.com
Printed in the USA
BVHW030822251119
564755BV00006B/92/P